ALEX WAGNER

THE GRAVE IN THE DUNES

A Case for the Master Sleuths

1

The North Sea island of Sylt may not have been Alaska, but it was definitely the second best place for a Malamute like me. As a proud descendant of the great Arctic wolves, I loved nothing more than to roam the island's dune landscapes in cold stormy weather, even if some areas were unfortunately closed to dogs. By now I was really familiar with the trails that were open to me, and whenever the opportunity arose I took a walk, enjoying the salty breeze in my nose and the soft sand and grass under my paws.

Sometimes Victoria Adler, my human, and my cat friend, Pearl, would accompany me, but by now it was November and they preferred to stay in the comfortably-heated parlor.

The tiny one, Pearl, was actually also a daughter of the High North, but a dyed-in-the-wool sofa cat by conviction, and Victoria like all humans had no fur worth mentioning and was forced to wrap herself in thick clothing every time she wanted to go outside. Poor, pitiful two-leggeds—one could really feel sorry for them.

Victoria often didn't lock the front door when we were home, because Sylt is generally a safe and peaceful place, at least as far as burglaries are concerned.

There is little theft, but when it comes to murder I cannot in good conscience call the island a secure refuge. Pearl and I had recently had to solve a series of murders in the very abode in which we were now living.

The fact that Victoria still felt safe enough to often leave the front door unlocked was probably due to me. I am actually a sled dog by nature, but since Victoria had become my human and Pearl my cat, I took good care of the two of them. It has been a point of honor, even if it is a full-time job. Pulling sleds would be much easier.

Be that as it may, the unlocked front door allowed me to push down the handle myself, using a few acrobatics and my pawing skills, and so I could get out into the open whenever I pleased. In this way I was able to undertake unsupervised wanderings, both near to and further from the house. I usually preferred to roam around at night, as most people disappeared into their houses and slept, and Sylt almost turned into an untouched wilderness even though the island was small and quite densely populated in some parts. In November far fewer tourists come to the island, and that was just fine with me.

On this particular day I had already walked a good distance on my nocturnal hike. I was enjoying the boundless freedom, the loneliness of the dune landscape and the seemingly endless starry sky above me. Perhaps I am a little bit romantically inclined, I will admit: more aesthete and thinker than hunter and killer, even if some murderer is constantly crossing my otherwise peaceful path and the wolf in me must go into action.

I trotted along lost in thought, following one or another of the dune dwellers' scent trails—who had long since sought the distance when a dog of my size approached them—but on the whole I was just letting myself drift wherever my paws took me.

However, I suddenly perceived movement out of the corner of my eye. I immediately came to a halt, pricked up my ears, sniffed and slowly turned my head.

I had not been mistaken; behind a high tuft of grass I spotted a shadow that had just taken cover there.

It was not a human. The smell that my nose detected was not familiar to me, but in the next moment my eyes revealed what my olfactory organ could not determine—for suddenly, as if from nowhere, a stately fox stood before me.

No wonder my nose had failed me. I'd had no idea how foxes smelled in practice, because I had never actually met one. Like most other animals that crawled and flew on our planet, I knew these not-so-distant cousins only from nature documentaries on television.

This specimen was a friendly guy, it seemed to me, but obviously I was scaring him.

He put back his ears and pulled in his tail.

"Hello there, dog," he greeted me, "there's enough for both of us, so no need to get bent out of shape.

We'll share, alright? He's still fresh."

At first I didn't quite understand what he was on about, but then I realized that he was standing on a flat mound of sand in which he had apparently been digging. And in doing so he had undoubtedly made a momentous discovery, because directly beside the fox a human hand was protruding from the earth!

I could not believe my eyes. As something of a canine historian I was of course aware that people had lived in Sylt since time immemorial; I also knew that long, long ago they had interred their dead in burial mounds, the remains of which could still be seen scattered here and there in the landscape of the dunes.

But the grave that lay before me now could not have originated from prehistoric times. The fox had been correct in what he'd said earlier: the two-legged who lay buried here was still quite fresh. Now at last the smell of the corpse rose to my nostrils. It was not as strong as that of the fox, but nevertheless clearly perceptible.

The human had definitely been male, judging by the size of the hand, and he did not yet smell of advanced decay. The skin on his fingers—at least in the moonlight—still looked like that of a living man, rosy and smooth. All right, maybe a tiny bit gray, not completely rosy, but—

"Help me dig it out," the fox said, snapping me out of my musings. "Then we'll share the spoils, okay? Very fraternally—fifty-fifty."

Where a wild animal had picked up a term like *fifty-*

fifty, which somehow sounded like a gangster in a low budget TV-movie to my ears, was beyond me.

Unfortunately I did not get to ask him about it, because while he was still talking to me he was already pushing his front paws into the sand in order to further expose the corpse.

He was an excellent digger, I noted appreciatively—and I know what I'm talking about. I can definitely call myself an expert in the field of excavation, because my whole life I have loved to dig, even though I haven't been able to inspire Victoria or Pearl with any enthusiasm for this high art.

For a moment I just stood there and marveled at the fox's excellent technique. The sand splattered behind him while his front paws dug evenly and relentlessly into the earth like a front-end loader. Within moments he'd uncovered the entire forearm of the dead man.

In my defense, I must say that I was a bit slow on the uptake. I was completely baffled by such an unexpected find; otherwise I would have intervened sooner. However I eventually remembered that I was not only an accomplished digger but above all a now very experienced four-pawed detective, and finally snapped out of it.

"Stop—stop!" I yelped. "We can't just eat this body. If a human really has been secretly buried here, it's a case for the police ... and we can't destroy this crime scene. Let alone damage the corpse! I'm sorry, but you'll just have to find another meal. Don't foxes prefer fresh meat, in any case?" I added. I wanted to show him that although I might be only a pet, I had some idea of the culinary customs of the wild.

The fox appeared completely unimpressed. "Isn't your nose working, bro? It's fresh!" he explained to me patiently.

Bro? The fox was clearly consuming some kind of TV offering somewhere, and not high quality programming either. So much for being a wild animal....

"I bet this guy has been dead for less than a whole day," he explained to me enthusiastically. "And now here he is, perfectly preserved thanks to the cold. A real feast, dude! Besides, I've never tasted a two-legged before. I bet you haven't either, have you?"

"No—um, I'm sorry, but we won't be tasting it today either," I said firmly.

I had not the slightest desire to sample human flesh, apart from the fact that this corpse was not to be eaten. I took a step towards the fox.

Of course I didn't intend to threaten him, but only to prevent him from nibbling on the corpse. For one thing was clear to me: if the two-leggeds had secretly buried one of their own in the sand of the dunes here, then it was certainly not a lawful interment.

People who died of natural causes could be laid to rest in cemeteries or cremated for all I cared, but certainly not hidden in the sand in the middle of the island wilderness. Barrow burials have been out of fashion for millennia.

I was pretty sure that the fox had stumbled upon a

murder victim, and fortunately I knew just the right man to look at the corpse: Chief Inspector Oskar Nüring, who headed up Sylt's criminal investigation department and who we had only recently encountered during our first murder case here on the island. Our first and apparently far from final murder case, I should say.

In the meantime Oskar had also become Victoria's good friend on a personal level, and Pearl and I liked him just as much.

I groaned inwardly. I had been so looking forward to a few peaceful weeks of vacation here on the island, and now I had come across yet another dead person who had certainly not died a natural death.

Corpses always lined our path, as Pearl was fond of putting it, in her strikingly inimitable style. She *loves* to solve murders, but my inclinations are less morbid by far.

But this didn't help me now, for the feast that the fox had so generously wanted to share with me had been the victim of a violent crime. There was no getting around that.

It was enough to drive me crazy, chasing my own tail.

2

Leading Oskar Nüring to the corpse before the little vulpine gourmand made it into a midnight feast and destroyed important trace evidence in the process was no easy task.

I first had to explain to this allegedly wild animal, who'd clearly enjoyed too many gangster movies, that this was a murder case and that the two-legged responsible had to be found and punished.

"Oh man, bro, are you a police dog or something?" he asked me.

"I, um—something like that, yes," I replied. There was no time for long-winded explanations right now, and anyway it was actually somehow true.

Of course I am not officially in the service of the police; I'd be the first and only law-enforcement Malamute if that were so. For some reason the humans in the police service prefer shepherd dogs, whether German or Belgian. Most unfair, but there's nothing I can do about it. These four-pawed colleagues of mine—or should I say *bros*?—might be faster and more agile than a sled dog like me, and perhaps a touch better at sniffing, but it's the inner strengths that matter, I would say. I am certainly no coward, and my little gray cells are more than a match for those of the Alsatians and Malinois.

I am, after all, a four-pawed detective who has already put several murderers behind bars, and few police dogs can claim *that*.

"Cool, dude!" the fox said enthusiastically. I made a deal with him: I promised to bring him some very special delicacies from Victoria's pantry at the first opportunity. I held out the prospect of dainties that no fox on Sylt had ever tasted, on the condition that he not only leave the corpse untouched, but also guard it carefully until my return. The smell of the dead body, now partially unearthed, would certainly attract other hungry creatures from the nocturnal animal kingdom. And I had to walk quite a distance back to Victoria's house, where I would hopefully be able to make contact with Inspector Nüring.

Strictly speaking, it wasn't actually Victoria's house. We were only guests here on Sylt, and the villa actually belonged to an animal psychologist and her loquacious parrot, who were off on a long trip at the moment—but that didn't matter now. I turned and ran, galloping back home as fast as my paws would carry me, and slipped through the front door, which I opened for myself again. Then I barked Victoria and Pearl out of their deep, peaceful sleep.

Both were less than enthusiastic about the late-night disturbance.

"Athos, are you out of your mind?" gasped Victoria as I slapped my wet tongue against her ear to finally get her out of bed. "What on earth is wrong?"

Okay, admittedly the tip of my tongue might have

even landed *in* her ear and sprayed a little saliva in there, but it is the fastest way to awaken your human. Secretly I suspect that my infamous ear kisses could even wake the dead. Perhaps I should test this theory on one of the innumerable corpses that drop before the paws of the tiny one and me.

Pearl looked rumpled and sleepy, and at first yawned at me so prodigiously that I was forced to stare deep into her miniature fanged maw.

But when I told her about the grave concealed in the dunes, and that the dead man was undoubtedly a murder victim, she was immediately wide awake. As I've already said, murders are her great passion, as macabre as that might sound regarding a seemingly cute and innocent kitten.

Of course, appearances are deceptive in her case—very much so. Pearl's adorable looks and the guileless expression she can adopt in a split second are merely weapons in her arsenal. They are used whenever she has once again committed some grave sin in the eyes of our humans—or when she's determined to bend some unwitting two-legged to her will as a devoted slave.

Cats ... need I say more?

It took Victoria quite a while to realize that I wanted her to follow me out into the night. The distance we had to cover was so far that she almost turned back two or three times before we finally reached the place where the body lay.

Pearl generously allowed Victoria to carry her all the

way, but kept asking me questions about the dead man that I of course couldn't answer.

"Who was this two-legged whose grave the fox discovered?" she wanted to know.

"How could I possibly tell from his hand or forearm?" I objected.

"Was it definitely a man, and not a woman?"

No idea why the pipsqueak found that so important.

"How was he murdered?"

"It's not like his right arm was chopped off," I replied.

"And what was he doing in this *ice desert* in the middle of the night?"

I saved my breath and didn't point out that Sylt was not an ice desert, and neither was it the forecourt of hell, as Pearl so liked to portray it. Just because she was such an effeminate sofa-loving kitty, who froze her plush little butt off if a fresh breeze so much as came up.

Half an eternity had passed before I could finally guide my two-legged and Madame Sofa Cat—who was perched on Victoria's arm like a king's daughter on her throne—to the grave site. Fortunately I have an excellent sense of direction. Once or twice I had to cheat a little, admittedly, and sniff out my own scent trail to find my way—but hey, it's the result that counts, right?

Victoria meanwhile was annoyed that I was leading her a merry dance through the cold night air. She tried several times to catch up with me and put on my leash, no doubt intending to drag me back to the warm house, but I managed to elude her quite cleverly.

In the end I knew she would realize what I was trying to do with this night's outing, and I was already picturing the juicy steak I aimed to receive as my reward when it became clear that I'd tracked down a murder victim.

The fox made off before Victoria could catch a glimpse of him. Silently, like a phantom, he disappeared into the high dune grasses.

As he melted into the darkness, he called out to me, "Don't forget our deal, my dude! Or have you brought me my feast right away?" After he had taken cover, and only his two shining eyes were staring out of the grass in our direction, he added, "I've never tasted cat either, you know—there's a lot of them here on the island, but they're damned defensible little beasts, I tell you. Do they taste good?"

Honestly, my fellow creatures' logic wasn't really operating tonight. "You think I'd eat cats if I lived with one, *bro*?" I replied.

Pearl, confident as she ever was when sitting on Victoria's arm or hiding behind me, hissed down at our friendly gourmet from above.

"Watch out, she can breathe fire," I murmured to the fox, so quietly that the tiny one wouldn't hear me.

"Whew," he said. "I'll get out of your hair, then. But I'll see you again, right? So we can feast together!"

"I promise," I said, and with that my distant cousin disappeared.

I guided Victoria the last few steps to the arm of the poor devil I'd seen lying dead under the sand.

She was startled at first and clapped her hand over her mouth, which almost knocked Pearl off her perch. She was reprimanded for this outrage with another loud hiss.

"Sorry, sweetie," Victoria managed, distractedly.

She set the tiny one down on the dirty ground, then took a deep breath and stared more closely at the arm, which stood out chalk-white against the light brown of its sandy grave. She kept a safe distance from it, obviously not feeling the need to touch it or disturb it further.

Like Pearl and me, she was not facing her first murder victim here, so she finally did what I had hoped she would do: she dug her cell phone out of her jacket pocket and called Oskar Nüring.

Less than half an hour later the inspector appeared on the scene, Victoria having sent him our exact location via cell phone. The two-leggeds have no sense of smell worth mentioning and are terrible trackers, but they know how to compensate for this shortcoming in part via the use of their advanced technology.

It wasn't long after the Chief Inspector's arrival in the dunes that more and more of his colleagues began showing up at the scene of the crime. Soon the lonely coastal landscape was swarming with humans who all seemed to know exactly what they had to do. Lamps were set up, barrier tapes stretched out, and people began digging while chatting excitedly with each other and snapping lots of photos.

Oskar stood a bit apart from them with the three of us, and let Victoria describe how she had found the body. She didn't adorn herself with other people's laurels, but truthfully reported that I had tracked down the corpse myself. Of course, she couldn't know anything about *bro* fox and the fact that the credit actually belonged to him.

"Good dog," Oskar said kindly. He got down on his knees, scratched me behind the ears and bravely endured me giving him an excited wet kiss—this time on the nose and not on one of his ears. I save the ears for emergencies.

I wagged my tail and panted cheerfully. "You're very welcome. That'll be one big juicy steak, please," I quipped, but of course I was not understood as usual.

Fortunately, neither Victoria nor Oskar thought to question the reason for my nightly excursion, which had so fortuitously led to my discovery of the corpse.

Victoria was a psychotherapist, originally of humans but recently also of quadrupeds, and therefore thought often about the souls of humans and animals. She liked to talk about the fact that all creatures—no matter how many legs, wings or fins they might have—needed their own space to grow and thrive in life.

Therefore she usually turned a blind eye when I secretly stole out of the house, or escaped from my leash while on a walk. After all, she knew that I could take care of myself and would always find my way back to her and to my little pipsqueak.

"Look, Athos, over there!" Pearl shouted suddenly.

I turned my head to follow her gaze.

3

Oskar's team had already uncovered most of the grave, and now I saw two forensics workers, looking like aliens in their white paper-thin coveralls, documenting the body and its location.

But Pearl drew my attention to a third two-legged. He was standing a few steps away from the dead man and ruffling his wildly tousled hair, which was peeking out from under a pointed cap. His tresses had the same color as the fur of *bro* fox.

For a crazy moment, I almost thought my new vulpine friend had turned into a human. You saw such shape shifters on the two-leggeds' television shows quite often lately—in fact, just a few days ago Pearl and I had watched several such fantasy movies with Victoria, in which the humans had turned into wolves. Only to fight vampires, of all things.

I have no idea what the two-legged who was responsible for the script had been thinking. And although the wolves were big, imposing and brave—much like I imagined my Alaskan ancestors to be—the leading lady of the films had ended up marrying one of the vampires. What an extraordinary aberration of taste!

I knew, of course, that in real life one needn't fear to meet such shapeshifters, whether they be wolves or island foxes with a penchant for gangster vernacular. I was probably just in a very strange mood, in view of the fact that we once again had to deal with a corpse.

The two-legged with the fox-colored hair, who was standing apart from the others where no spotlight fell, seemed to be in great emotional turmoil. He jumped from one leg to the other, grimaced in pain, and did not stop pulling his own hair. He seemed to be moaning and complaining, even though I couldn't hear exactly what he was saying.

The crime scene investigators paid no attention to him, but when I looked more closely I felt my jaw drop open. The human I was staring at was only a child, who could be no older than seven or eight years of age. He was small, undernourished and dressed rather like a little vagrant. A plaid wool shirt, but no jacket—in this cold?—green pants and brown boots.

I was looking at the boy only in profile, but even so I noticed that he had rather large ears protruding from under his pointed cap. Again I was reminded of the fox....

The eyes were just as large as my distant cousin's, but the boy had a tiny snub nose that rivaled Pearl's.

Maybe he had a genetic peculiarity like Pearl, too? She would always look like a kitten, even though she had long been an adult cat and could act like a full-grown tiger when something went against her grain—so quite often, in other words.

This boy looked equally peculiar; small, childlike, yet somehow ... not. I can't describe it any better than that.

Well in truth his appearance was not so very important—much more decisive was the question of to whom the child *belonged*. Certainly not to *bro* fox.

He seemed to be afraid. Or did he feel somehow responsible for the death of the man who had been buried here in the sand?

It couldn't be.

I thought that it was great and very progressive of Victoria to let me roam around out here at night by myself. I loved having this personal freedom, to which she also attached so much value. But a small child, out by himself in the middle of a November night, in the loneliness of the Sylt dunes? That was dangerous! The hackles on the back of my neck stood on end at the thought of what might happen to the helpless little human out here alone and with no fur to protect him.

A terrible thought came to me: did the boy possibly belong to the murder victim? Had this man, whom not even a sloppy wet ear kiss could recall from the realm of the dead, and who was now the focus of our investigation and surrounded by suit-clad forensics examiners, been the father of this strange boy? Had the poor little kid possibly been a witness to his murder, and was he now tormenting himself with feelings of guilt because he had not been able to protect his father?

I wanted to walk right over to the little one and comfort him, but I was uncomfortably aware that a dog of my size could not simply run up to such a youngster, who seemed already half out of his mind with grief.

The boy might well have fallen over with fright.

So I set off towards him slowly and carefully, but Pearl had no such qualms. She is a pipsqueak herself and, as I've noted, blessed with the most innocent and harmless appearance. So she straight away toddled up to the little one, with her snub nose curiously protruding, and meowed softly.

I expected that—despite his visibly agitated state—he would manage a small smile as soon as he caught sight of the tiny one, and that he would then pick Pearl up and cuddle her. Just about every two-legged was prone to do that when they first laid eyes on her, after all. Of course she doesn't grant this favor to everyone, but is extremely picky about who is allowed to mess up her silky white fur. But I don't think I need to mention that.

If the wrong two-legged touches her, or she just doesn't feel like being stroked, you'd catch a scratched nose faster than you can say *Ouch!*

I speak from experience; Pearl likes to use me as a pillow, but woe betide me if I ever let my muzzle droop onto one of *her* paws, and she isn't in the mood....

But the boy did not react as I had predicted. He did not smile, nor did he seem to have the slightest interest in petting Pearl. He did gaze at her for a brief moment, as if he were looking at something wondrous and exotic—but then he simply vanished.

In a flash he scurried away, and the next moment he had disappeared into the tall grasses between the dunes.

I could still smell him, but in the darkness I could no longer make him out, and I had to marvel again.

He didn't smell like a child at all, but rather like a much older person. I perceived aromas of straw and grain, of flowers and wood. However, unlike most two-leggeds, the little one did not smell of soap or shampoo at all. Apparently he did not like to bathe.

I turned to Pearl. "Where did he go?" I asked her.

She narrowed her eyes. "I don't know, but he's fast as hell. For a human."

She braced herself against a gust of wind that swept by overhead and ruffled her fur. "Brr, what nasty weather," she whimpered. "This ice desert really is a terrible place to die."

"Your ancestors—" I began, but she cut me off.

"They came from Russia, I know. But I'm just more..."

"...of a sofa cat?"

She hissed, which was probably meant to seem threatening.

Then she went on, "But honestly, Athos, another murder case for us to work on? This time it's happened particularly quickly after the last one. It seems to me that this island isn't just the forecourt of hell, as far as the weather is concerned, but downright life-threatening. At least for two-leggeds."

We turned around and retraced the few steps that separated us from Oskar and Victoria. There the next surprise already awaited us.

"He was definitely murdered," Oskar was just telling our human. "Two stab wounds to the chest."

Of course we were not surprised about *that* fact, seeing as we'd already concluded that the poor man could not have died a natural death. The hidden, isolated grave in the dunes, where he'd found his final resting place, spoke of this all too clearly.

Oskar's next words, however, were quite unexpected.

"I'm afraid I already know the identity of our victim," he said. "The description fits perfectly: about forty years old, white-blond chin-length hair, green eyes, and a hooked nose. That's not the kind of face you see often. Also about six foot tall and slightly chubby. That's about right; and just such a man was reported missing this very afternoon."

"By his family?" asked Victoria.

"No—by his client. The man's name was Edward Laymon, and he was a private investigator."

"Oh. That's definitely unusual," Victoria agreed. "And why was his customer so worried about him?"

"I don't know, exactly. I'll have to take a look into it first."

He frowned and buried his hands deeper into his jacket pockets.

"We may not have taken the report seriously enough," he went on. "You see, the detective's client in question, the one who called us, is a movie star. And while she seemed quite frightened, she couldn't—or more likely, wouldn't—tell us exactly why she thought something had happened to her private eye. My colleague, who was on telephone duty at the station, probably assumed that she was just a bit overexcited and was worried about the man for no good reason. Now I guess we'll have to ask more questions, even if it's too late for the poor devil."

"Do you blame yourself?" asked Victoria gently.

"No—I didn't know anything about it. And I don't really have anything to reproach my colleague on the desk for, either. The department is so understaffed at the moment due to illness that you have to set priorities, and fortunately the vast majority of missing persons cases are resolved in the end. Besides, if a detective goes offline for a few hours or goes into hiding—well, that could certainly have been for professional reasons."

"And for what purpose did the woman, this actress, hire Edward Laymon?" Victoria went on.

"I don't know that yet, either. She mentioned something to the desk sergeant about private research she had hired the detective to carry out, but that could mean anything. I will have to question her more closely now, too."

"Do you think he might have made a mortal enemy in the course of this research?" asked Victoria.

"Quite possibly, but then a private eye can have any number of enemies—which he may have made during other quite different assignments at any time in the past."

"And this actress ... does she live here on Sylt?"

"No, she's just vacationing on the island with the family. Her father-in-law is Steven Harrington, the famous hotelier—does that name mean something to you? He just bought a luxury resort here on the island to add to his consortium of premium hotels. It's where he's staying with his loved ones for the next few weeks."

"Steven Harrington? Oh my goodness—then the actress you're talking about is Julia Trapp? She is his daughter-in-law, isn't she? I'm quite a big fan of her movies."

Oskar nodded. "Yes, exactly."

"She's in a wheelchair, if I recall correctly," continued Victoria. "Some nasty accident a few years ago. It wasn't widely reported in the media at the time, as you'd expect with such a famous woman."

"A fall from a balcony, as far as I know," Oskar said. "There was radio silence for a year or two, but now she's in the public eye again. There are a lot of roles for paraplegics these days, especially as inclusion has become such an important issue."

Oskar looked down at Pearl and me. "I have a request for you, Victoria: do you think you could take your—um, co-therapists, and talk to Mrs. Trapp sometime tomorrow? I'll question her later, officially of course, but I'd also like your opinion as a psychologist on what has transpired. If you don't mind, of course. I haven't come across a murdered private detective in my entire career here, I have to say."

"Yes, no problem," Victoria said. "I'm happy to help."

She met my gaze, then Pearl's. "*We're* happy to help. I just can't believe we're meeting death again, Oskar—if I may put it that way. Our sixth actual murder case, albeit only the second one with you. It's really starting to creep me out."

Me too, Victoria, I thought silently. *Me too.*

4

Pearl and I ensured that Victoria would take us with her the next morning, as she'd agreed, when she met up with Oskar to go to the hotel where the famous actress was staying. We made ourselves snug in the entrance hall of the house, right by the front door, so that our two-legged would have no chance to leave without us.

As Oskar had told us earlier, Julia Trapp was staying in a luxury resort on the beach that her father-in-law had recently incorporated into his hotel chain, and which was now renamed the *Harrington Resort Sylt*. It consisted of a two-story main building with large picture windows, and several bungalows and villas grouped around it to imitate a loose little village community. One could not help but think of a kind of storybook settlement, nestled in the dunes and close to the beach. The facades of all the houses were whitewashed, and they had the thatched roofs that are so popular on Sylt.

Thatch is dried reeds, which are nicely cut into shape and replace the otherwise normal roof tiles. It insulates well and looks really homely.

Between the villas and around the main building a garden had been laid out, with a meticulously mowed lawn and many flower beds, in which some frost-resistant plants still persevered even so late in the year. In addition, there were a few tall trees and a wide variety of ornamental shrubs, which were as foreign to Sylt as I was, but probably also enjoyed the harsh island climate. Not a withered leaf lay anywhere on the ground; a whole allotment of gardeners must have been active in the hotel complex. The humans like it clean and tidy, especially here in northern Germany.

Julia Trapp, together with her caregiver, her husband and his secretary, were living in one of the largest villas in the complex. It was a mighty two-story building in which a large family could have lived all year round, and not just on vacation.

Inside, everything was decorated with light woods and fabrics, and it looked even more neat and tidy than in the garden space.

The actress and her caregiver, a certain André Meissner, welcomed us into a spacious ground floor living room with floor-to-ceiling French windows that led out onto a terrace.

Oskar introduced Victoria as a psychological consultant he had officially brought in for the murder case, and Victoria in turn presented us to the actress as her emotional support co-workers.

Julia Trapp seemed deeply disturbed. One might have assumed that someone particularly close to her had died, but perhaps she was simply a very sensitive soul and took the sudden and brutal demise of her private detective very much to heart.

Pearl began the poor woman's therapy with a round

of kitty cuddles, which almost never failed to have its desired effect. Julia sat in her wheelchair, her nurse André standing by her side as a devoted valet, ready to read her glance and fulfill her every wish. Pearl brought a smile to the faces of both two-leggeds when she nimbly jumped onto the actress's lap and settled down there after circling twice to get comfortable.

Julia could not move her legs, but her upper body was quite strong to make up for it—especially her arms. Nevertheless, she did not appear overly muscular, but rather she was a fairly petite and somehow fragile-looking woman.

I estimated her to be in her early forties, although I am not necessarily an expert in determining the ages of two-leggeds. With time one gets an approximate feeling for these things, however.

She smelled of a floral perfume. I sniffed out jasmine, which almost took my breath away, combined with a dusky rose scent. Julia wore sparkling jewels on her ears and neck, and had bright green eyes and black curly hair that fell over her shoulders.

André Meissner, on the other hand, was dressed quite simply: a turtleneck sweater and jeans, and sports shoes. He was certainly five or ten years younger than his patient, and he was powerfully built, appearing very athletic. His hair reminded me of a golden retriever, wispy and light blond.

It seemed Julia Trapp was a very well-known actress, even though I hadn't seen any of her movies yet. Victoria confessed that she was a big fan of her romantic dramas. "Even though we've been watching almost nothing but crime procedurals and thrillers lately," she added, lost in thought. "You won't believe this, but my cat won't watch anything else—and she runs the show at our house."

Of course, Julia and André didn't believe her. Both laughed—André quite animatedly, and Julia, on the other hand, only quietly and somehow melancholically. Clearly they couldn't imagine the kind of bloodthirsty creature that was hiding behind the sweet-kitten facade. Only I knew the true depth of the abyss.

Pearl always insisted that a television program focused on murder or manslaughter was essential to building up our detective skills, and good-natured dog as I am, I watched along with her.

She acknowledged Victoria's admission that she was the one in charge at our house with a sympathetic purr, and instead of contradicting her I saved my breath. In truth I am the leader of our pack! A forty-five-kilogram almost-wolf wouldn't be subdued by a half-pint cat, now would he?

"I am truly honored to meet you, Mrs. Trapp," Victoria continued, "even though the circumstances of our acquaintance are so dire. I think I've seen every one of your films, and I've always been impressed by how you portray even the most difficult characters so convincingly."

Julia was probably used to such compliments. She smiled bravely, even though she continued to look as if she had one foot in the grave herself. Under the strong floral scent she had put on, she clearly smelled too much of fear for my taste. I was dying to know why the death of the detective was so upsetting to her—or was there something more behind her anxiety?

"Please, do call me Julia," she replied wanly, stroking Pearl's fur.

"Victoria," our human replied in kind, gently touching the actress's arm.

Julia's breathing definitely became calmer while Pearl purred devotedly, and Oskar saw his chance to ask her some necessary questions about the murdered detective who had been working on Sylt on her behalf.

"Who knew you had hired Edward Laymon?" Oskar wanted to know. "Did you meet with him here at the hotel?"

Julia nodded. "Not here in our villa—but in the tea room in the main building. There's hardly anything going on there, you know, because the hotel is generally only lightly booked this time of year. Only real nature lovers come to Sylt in the winter, it seems to me."

Again she tried to smile, which looked almost genuine, but I attributed that more to her acting ability. She still seemed tense, her shoulders hunched, and not even Pearl's cuddle therapy had been able to calm her down completely.

"And who was present at this conversation in the tea room?" asked the Chief Inspector. "Besides you, of course?"

"Just André. I pretty much go nowhere without him.

He's my factotum, in a way. He's absolutely indispensable."

The orderly inclined his head as if to thank her for the praise he'd received.

"Did you tell anyone else about the meeting?" inquired Oskar. "Or talk generally to someone about hiring a detective? With your husband, perhaps, or another family member?"

"A strange question, Chief Inspector," she replied. She pressed herself against the back of her wheelchair. "I didn't say anything to anyone—but you're not seriously suggesting that someone in my family did something to him, are you?"

"Of course not," Oskar said quickly. "But we have to consider all the possibilities. I'm sure you understand that."

Then he continued, "I would like to come back to the reason you engaged Mr. Laymon's services. You mentioned something yesterday about private research that you hired him to do. Could you please elaborate on that a little bit? What was his exact job, and why did he come here to the hotel?"

Julia straightened her back even more, which made her look slightly taller. She also seemed to have finally shaken off her trepidation, at least to some extent. Her voice sounded determined, more self-confident.

"I hired Mr. Laymon to do a background check on an applicant for an assistant position with me. I need to trust this person with important business and financial matters, so I wanted to have her screened before I hire her."

"And that's why you asked your detective to come to your vacation home?" said Oskar. It was obvious that to him the explanation seemed rather strange—to me, too, by the way.

"Our main residence is in Hamburg, so it's only a few hours away from here by car, and Mr. Laymon was based there as well, so he didn't have to travel far to get here either. Because I'm on vacation, I've simply had leisure to focus my attention on the matter. My everyday life can sometimes get a bit hectic, what with my shooting schedule and all that goes along with it. Still—or precisely because of that—I wanted to hire a new assistant quickly. That's all."

"Nevertheless, it seems strange to me that Mr. Laymon would have taken a room here at the hotel," Oskar insisted. "Or was that your express wish?" He spoke kindly and gently, but kept up the pressure.

But Julia only shrugged her shoulders. "I'm afraid I can't say anything about his motives for doing so, Chief Inspector," she said stiffly.

"Your candidate he was supposed to be checking out doesn't live here on Sylt, I take it?"

"No—she's also in Hamburg."

"I understand. Please make a note of her name for me, as we need to check if she might have had something to do with Mr. Laymon's death."

Julia furrowed her brow. "You're not serious, are you? You don't kill someone just because you might have told a few white lies on your résumé."

Oskar Laymon pulled a small notebook and pen from his inside jacket pocket. "The woman's name, please?"

"I'll have to check my records," Julia Trapp said. "I'll get the precise information to you."

Oskar nodded silently, but did not take his eyes off her.

Pearl gave me a meaningful look from the actress's lap. "Something's not quite right here," she said in the tone of a seasoned criminologist. "This woman is hiding something, or does it just seem that way to me? Oskar clearly doesn't trust her."

"I have that impression, too," I said. "But what could she possibly have to hide? And why? I can hardly believe she went to the dunes in her wheelchair to kill the detective, or at any rate to dispose of his body. That would never have worked. That thing she's in isn't some sort of SUV."

"She wouldn't be the first to have faked an illness," Pearl opined. "We've seen that often in mysteries, haven't we?" The knowing look she gave me was probably meant to mean, "There, you see how important it is to choose the right television program? We could never have learned such things from romantic dramas."

Oskar stood up and put his notebook carefully away. He said goodbye to Mrs. Trapp for the present and promised to return once his investigation was fully underway.

"We'll have more questions for you soon," he explained, unapologetically.

When we were standing outside the villa again—Oskar, Victoria, Pearl and me—he turned to us with a frown. "Well, I'm willing to bet my right hand that that woman didn't tell us everything she knows. Actress or not, she wasn't honest with me. Besides, I got the strong impression at first that she was scared—although that could be due to all sorts of reasons, of course. And all too understandable when you're being questioned by the major crime squad."

"It seemed to me that she was lying to us, too," Victoria said.

Oskar pulled his scarf tighter around his neck and scowled forbiddingly. "Well, we'll see—we'll get to the truth all right. For now, I'll take a closer look at the dead man's background, reconstruct his steps here on the island. The usual routine. I'll call you, okay?"

"Sure," Victoria said.

"You and me, Athos, we're going to have to solve this thing," Pearl said cat-pertly. "That's what it boils down to, doesn't it? As always."

5

Victoria had forgotten to put a leash on us, and instead of walking straight back to her car she just wandered aimlessly among the bungalows and villas of the hotel complex for quite some time.

She was probably paying no heed whatsoever to the level of dedication and work that had to go into this perfect green oasis every day, because her gaze was entirely blank and she seemed to be entertaining dark thoughts. I assumed they revolved around Julia Trapp and her murdered detective.

At some point Victoria stopped short, looked down at us and said, "I need to gain Julia's trust, I think—maybe then she'll tell us more. I'm so sure she knows something she doesn't want to reveal to Oskar. But maybe she will to me, and that could certainly bring us a step further in our search for Edward Laymon's murderer. Don't you think so?"

"Definitely," I replied, wagging my tail vigorously to lend emphasis to my assertion.

"I agree," Pearl said. Her bushy little tail also bobbed back and forth for a brief moment, believe it or not.

I had observed this gesture, quite atypical for a cat, on her part on one or two occasions recently. Surely I wasn't rubbing off on her and *dogifying* her, of all people—who prided herself so definitively on her feline nature? So to speak.

The idea amused me, I must confess. This proved clearly that *I am* the leader of our pack, and Pearl sees me as a role model, as is only natural.

Of course, both my and Pearl's response eluded Victoria as usual, despite the emphatic wagging of my tail. But at least she understood that we were of one mind.

"Winning Julia's trust—that's probably best left to me," Pearl added, confident as ever.

The next moment she had already made a U-turn and toddled away on her tiny creamy-white paws, back in the direction of Julia's villa.

"We'll have to take a good look around the place and meet the family," she explained over her shoulder, expecting me to follow her as a matter of course.

"Wait a minute, not so fast," I urged her.

Mercifully, she actually stopped and turned toward me, albeit with her whiskers twitching impatiently.

"Look around the place? How exactly are you going to do that?" I asked—being the sensible, realistically inclined half of our duo. "How are we supposed to get back into the house? Do we just stroll in the door and settle down in Julia's house, or how do you envision doing it?"

"Why not? Surely no one is going to let a poor little kitten freeze to death on their doorstep in this cold weather."

"You are not poor, nor will you freeze," I objected. "Your fur is almost as thick as mine. And as for me, I don't think anyone would believe I'm cold."

"I can *look* cold and poor, though," Pearl said unabashedly. "And that's all that matters. If they don't let you in, you can wait for me and I'll report back to you later, all right? Oh, look—here comes our chance already. Come on, get your paws moving, Athos!"

I turned my head in the direction Pearl was facing and saw a woman who must be working for the hotel's room service. She was pushing a serving trolley ahead of her, on which there were several plates covered with steel domes. And she was moving her small catering cart precisely in the direction of the villa where Julia Trapp lived. How incredibly convenient!

"Come on," Pearl hissed at me, and scurried behind the woman along the garden path she had just turned into.

"Pearl! Stay with me!" Victoria shouted after her. "Where are you going?"

Once again I had to take it upon myself to make it clear to our two-legged what the plan was. Pearl rarely deigned to care about such—in her eyes unimportant—details.

I stepped stoutly in Victoria's way, barked once, and walked a bit toward her to make it clear that we now had to take matters into our own paws, and she should go away.

"Stick around, okay?" I said. "And pick us up again in a couple of hours. We'll do a little spying on Julia Trapp and her family—*undercover*, you know."

It wasn't just *bro* fox, who probably went in and out

of people's homes secretly somewhere and watched gangster movies, who knew how to express himself in a cool and casual way; I could do it too. However, I'd forgotten once again that it was a wasted effort to try to communicate with Victoria. She just saw her dog standing in front of her, panting at her and wagging its tail excitedly.

People....

As was only to be expected, Victoria looked at me in great puzzlement. In the meantime, the lady from room service had arrived at the door of Julia's villa with her serving trolley and pressed the bell.

André opened the door and greeted the woman, whom he had probably been expecting. Presumably he had placed a food order for himself and Julia.

He stepped aside and allowed the hotel employee to push her cart into the house. Pearl zoomed into the front room behind the woman in a flash.

André laughed. "Oh hey, kiddo, where are you going?"

Both he and the waitress turned to stare after Pearl, who had long since disappeared somewhere inside the villa, and thus they were facing away from me.

It was now or never; this was my chance to get into the house. And it was absolutely necessary, because I could not leave the tiny one to investigate on her own. She had a talent for maneuvering herself into perilous situations from which I always needed to rescue her at the very last minute. And for which I usually received zero recognition, let alone thanks.

I barked at Victoria once more, and wagged my tail to let her know that there was no need to worry. Then I went full throttle along the path and stormed through the open door, past André and the woman from room service. Arriving in the villa's vestibule, I dug in my claws to put on the brakes and looked around for Pearl. Unfortunately it's possible that in the process I scratched a bit of the parquet floor, which was spotless and looked very expensive. It was so embarrassing, but luckily neither of the two humans noticed.

But the woman from room service let out a scream. Not because of the floor, fortunately, but simply because I had given her a huge fright.

"Oh God, what kind of monster is this? Is this dog yours? He's huge."

Monster was hurtful and really not necessary—just because I am a bit bigger than Pearl.

But André took it upon himself to defend my honor. "Oh, don't worry," he said, undaunted. "These two, the dog and the kitten that just ran in here, actually visited us earlier, with ... an acquaintance," he quickly improvised.

He clearly didn't feel like telling the waitress more about Victoria's—and Oskar's—visit than was strictly necessary. He turned and looked out of the door into the open, presumably in search of Victoria.

I panted at him kindly and settled down on the damaged parquet floor, to signal that there was no danger from me but that at the same time I had come to stay.

Pearl was nowhere to be seen. Her scent trail led in the direction of the living room, where Julia Trapp had welcomed us earlier. She probably didn't want to lose any time in gaining the actress's trust, as she had so wholeheartedly promised.

6

It seemed Victoria had been smart enough not to follow me and had even disappeared from the villa's immediate vicinity. In any case André, who was still standing on the doorstep and looking around outside, couldn't spot her anywhere.

After a brief moment of perplexity, he turned to me and said, "Then you stay here with us, you two. Your mistress will show up again. Maybe she still has to do something with the Chief Inspector," he whispered to me with a conspiratorial grin.

"Thank you, that will be all," he said at a normal volume to the waitress, then pressed a tip into her hand and grabbed the handles of the small serving cart. The woman thanked him and disappeared—not without giving me an anxious look—before the door of the villa slammed shut behind her.

I followed André, who navigated with the trolley into the living room, and there I discovered Pearl and the actress. The tiny one had already made herself comfortable on Julia's lap, allowing herself to be cuddled, and was purring loudly. The actress was smiling blissfully with delight, her expression genuine now compared to our previous visit. It was just as I had expected; Pearl's cuteness factor could be relied upon after all.

"Isn't she just scrumptious?" Julia said to André, and the nurse-companion nodded with a smile.

"Oh, the dog is here too?" added Julia when she caught sight of me. "Is—that psychologist—?"

"No, I don't know where she's gone. She must be out somewhere in the hotel, and just letting her animals roam."

"And they both came right back to us?" said Julia with a beaming expression. "How sweet."

If you only knew, I thought to myself silently. *We are two spies whom you've unsuspectingly let into your house, a Trojan horse made not of wood, but unfortunately still amazingly good at scratching your innocent wooden floors.*

André removed the covers from the dishes on the trolley. Two portions of ham and eggs appeared, which he arranged on a small cozy table before he and Julia began to eat together. He was drinking from a mug of coffee, which he must have brewed himself in the kitchen, and she had a glass of orange juice. Neither of them seemed to be particularly hungry.

Pearl had hopped off Julia's lap because she would have been in the way during the meal, and had joined me on the floor.

"Hmm," she said, "I could do with a snack, too. What do you say we take a look around the kitchen and see if there's anything there for us?"

"We just had breakfast a few hours ago," I said. "You can't be hungry already, can you?"

Of course she could, the little glutton.

So we left the two-leggeds alone for the time being—they were busy eating anyway and so we didn't need to eavesdrop on their conversation.

From the foyer, we quickly found the villa's kitchen. You didn't have to be a master sleuth to do it, either.

The room was very small, which was probably due to the fact that we were in a hotel complex with room service, and not in a private home where you had to prepare every meal yourself.

Accordingly, and much to the chagrin of my little gourmand, there were no treats or any food at all to be seen. I cleverly opened a few of the lower cupboard doors with my muzzle, but even behind these there was only a yawning emptiness.

However, on the shelf between the stove and the sink there was a small porcelain bowl, which gave off a sweet, warm scent.

"What's in there, can you please check?" Pearl asked in a hopeful voice.

I rested my front paws on one of the base cabinets and peered into the bowl.

"Hmm, cereal porridge—doesn't look very inviting."

"Hey!" I heard Pearl exclaim behind me. "Hi, kiddo."

I dropped back onto all fours and looked at her. "Who are you talking to?"

Pearl turned her head toward the door. "Where has he gone, now? Just a moment ago he was—"

"Who, Pearl? There's no one here."

"The boy ... didn't you see him? No, how could you have? You were looking in the bowl. He came in the door just now, but as soon as he saw me he disappeared again. Pretty nimble for a human, especially for one so young."

She tiptoed out of the kitchen. I followed her, but I saw no one in the hallway.

"It was the same boy we saw last night," she explained to me. "I'm sure of it—out there in the ice desert, at the grave of that murdered detective."

"Are you certain?" I dared to ask.

Pearl wrinkled her nose in indignation. "Of course. What do you think? He had the same pointed hat, the same big eyes and ears—and he disappeared just as quickly as he did last night. It was him for sure."

"So where has he gone?"

"I don't know," Pearl said. "But he was here," she insisted.

It was on the tip of my tongue to say, "You're seeing ghosts," but I stifled the remark because I didn't feel like getting my nose scratched again. Pearl could be a sweet little kitten when she wanted to be, but she couldn't take the least bit of criticism. Typical cat. I decided I had to dogify her even further.

When I pressed my nose to the ground and sniffed around, I had the impression that I could make out the boy's scent—only very faintly, but it wasn't my imagination. But he had not left a real trail that I could have followed; it was almost as if he had disappeared into thin air right in front of our noses.

Great, I was smelling ghosts, too.

"Do you think the boy belongs to Julia?" Pearl mused

to herself. "Could he be her son?"

"Hmm, it's possible ... but then how did he escape the house last night without her or anyone else in here noticing?"

"Maybe he's a little adventurer who sneaks out of the villa at night," Pearl opined. "It's not too improbable. Certain dogs around here like to do it often." She gave me an amused look.

André then appeared in the hallway, and Madame Cat immediately saw her chance to grab a tidbit or two after all. She rubbed herself against the nurse-companion's ankles, meowed piteously as if she were about to die of hunger, and then ran straight back toward the kitchen.

Needless to say he followed her. She had the caregiver wrapped around her little paw in record time.

I joined the two of them and also trotted back into the kitchen. I am by no means a glutton like the tiny one, but fasting out of principle is also not my thing.

André went straight to the refrigerator and opened the door.

"Let's see if we have some sausage or something in here. Hmm."

There was milk and orange juice in the fridge, a cheese plate, some mini sausages, and handfuls of apples and tomatoes.

"I'm afraid we're not very well prepared for four-legged visitors, my little one," André said. "Let alone for ones who are so very hungry."

Pearl meowed again as if her life depended on it.

André withdrew his head from the refrigerator and cast a sidelong glance at the countertop, where the bowl of cereal porridge I had eyed earlier stood. He smiled and shook his head. Then he turned back to the refrigerator and reached in.

"Cheese or tomatoes are probably not your cup of tea, little lady, so I guess you'll have to make do with these sausages," he explained to Pearl. "They're from yesterday, as far as I know. I'm sure you'll like them, what do you think?"

He took the plate of sausages out of the refrigerator and placed it on the floor in front of Pearl.

"While not a huge portion," he said, "you are something of a miniature tiger."

The pipsqueak sniffed at the sausages.

"Bah. Don't they have any salmon here?" she whined. "I guess it's going to be a mission under the toughest conditions this time."

I refrained from commenting.

I'm dying of hunger, she'd said one moment. And the next—*but that? No, I'm not eating that.*

How do people put up with these cats?

7

"Let's go check on your mistress. I'm sure she's looking everywhere for you two cuties," André suggested, after I had taken pity on the two small sausages that Pearl had spurned. It would have been most rude to refuse André's kind offer, and there is always room in my stomach for a snack. Pearl really has no manners.

Apparently our spy mission was doomed to come to an early end. We didn't want to go straight back to Victoria; after all, we had come to snoop around here in the villa.

But of course, André was not supposed to know that, even if we could have made it clear to him.

So Pearl and I settled down with exaggerated tiredness on the kitchen floor after my little snack, pretending that we were in no condition to go looking for Victoria.

But André was unimpressed by our little show. He simply picked up Pearl, whose light weight was a real disadvantage in situations like these. By comparison, I am not carried away so easily if I make myself extra heavy.

She mewed in protest and extended her miniature claws, which I don't think André even noticed.

He ran with her into the anteroom and put on a jacket there that was hanging from the coat rack.

Without letting go of the tiny one, he simply shifted Pearl from one hand to the other as he slipped his arms into the jacket sleeves. Then he actually noticed her claws after all, and commented, "Oh, they are so cute. So tiny. You don't really want to tickle me, do you, little tiger?"

Pearl hissed indignantly, which only made his grin the wider.

Poor little thing. Her ego—normally the size of a saber-toothed tiger's—had taken a severe beating. One could almost have felt sorry for her. Almost.

Finally, André left the house with her in his arms. He moved at a fast clip; I had no choice but to trot after the two of them.

However, I couldn't help one little barb: "Sometimes it's quite advantageous if you weigh a little more and can't be carried off quite so easily," I said to Pearl. Although of course I am by no means fat. My splendid and very dense coat only adds a little to my girth.

She snorted.

"I'm not defenseless, if that's what you're thinking," she insisted. "I could bite him, after all, and then he'd let go of me instantly and I'd be back on the floor with you. However, we don't want to make ourselves unpopular, do we? We'll get back into the house all right, don't worry."

"I'm not worried," I replied. "I am a fearless Malamute."

Pearl's nose gave a telltale twitch. An unmistakable sign that she was enjoying herself.

It appeared that Victoria had actually stayed quite close by, just as I had instructed her to do. Sometimes it seemed she understood me quite well.

Anyway, she suddenly stepped out from behind a hedge not two minutes after we'd left Julia Trapp's villa, and acted delighted to see us again.

"Ah, here you are, you two little rascals!" she exclaimed in mock surprise. She gave André a big smile. "I was looking everywhere for these two. Did they run all the way back to your house?"

"Yes, exactly. They really are adorable, especially your miniature tiger. And of course we would have loved to keep them both with us, but I just didn't want you to worry."

"Very kind of you," Victoria said. When it came to winning the favor of complete strangers, she was second to none but Pearl herself.

André set the tiny one down gently and was about to leave, but Victoria stopped him, made some small talk about the island weather, and then cleverly involved him in conversation. Clearly she wanted to sound him out, which was just fine with me. When it comes to questioning—or even interrogating—the two-leggeds, we unfortunately have to rely on human help.

"I think it's impressive, the way you take care of Mrs. Trapp," she flattered him, with her most charming smile. "I have the impression that you are an invaluable help to her."

"I really hope so," André replied. "I've been with her for a couple of years—ever since she had that terrible accident."

Victoria nodded. Then she shifted from one foot to the other. "Look, André—I can call you André, can't I?"

"Sure."

"Thank you. My name is Victoria, but you already know that. What I want to say is, if you believe your employer may be in any kind of danger, please talk to me. She was very reluctant to speak to Chief Inspector Nüring, which I can understand. You just feel nervous when you're being questioned by the police, don't you? But this private detective that Mrs. Trapp hired was murdered in cold blood, and I can't help but feel that she's afraid of something—and that at the same time she's keeping something from us as well. I really don't want to imply anything; it's probably from the best of intentions. But her explanation as to why she engaged Mr. Laymon's services and had him check into the hotel—it didn't sound very convincing, to say the least. The Chief Inspector feels the same way. And you certainly wouldn't want Mrs. Trapp to put herself in unnecessary danger, would you?"—more charming smiles—"Whatever you confide in me, André, I would of course treat as private. I would keep it within the bounds of confidentiality as a therapist, if you will. So nothing would leak out anywhere..."

André raised his arms. "Yes, all right. I know you mean well, but..." He hesitated.

Victoria gave him a look that was almost as encouraging as my own, when I want to teach a human something important in the gentlest way.

"Well ... well," stammered André, "Mrs. Trapp did indeed fib a bit about the assignment she gave Edward Laymon. But there's nothing illegal behind it, I assure you. She was probably just embarrassed to talk to you about it."

"About what?" inquired Victoria.

"You promise you won't rat me out to Julia? I'm usually very discreet, you know, and she attaches great importance to that."

"My word of honor," Victoria promptly replied.

"All right—I trust you. So here's the deal. The truth is that she retained Mr. Laymon's services because she suspected her husband, Tristan Harrington, of infidelity. Mr. Laymon came to our hotel to give her a report on his investigation into the matter, and she then immediately instructed him to stay here and continue to carry out surveillance on Tristan."

"Did Mr. Laymon find out that Mr. Harrington was actually cheating, then?" asked Victoria.

"Oh yes, I'm afraid there's no doubt about that. The photographs he presented to Mrs. Trapp made it abundantly clear. But Julia—she doesn't want to admit how faithless her husband is, you know. Until now she has always preferred to look the other way, while Tristan is..."

He hesitated, and seemed to be searching for the right words. "Let's just say he's a notorious womanizer, and that's putting it kindly. Julia has been turning a blind eye to his extramarital affairs for years. No, both eyes. And I don't want to watch him break her heart—

but I guess I have no choice."

He sighed. "Be that as it may, she thought this time that Tristan's fling, which the detective told her about, might merely have been a one-night stand. So I suggested that Mr. Laymon check into the hotel and gather more evidence over the following few days, to see whether the relationship would continue or not."

He twisted his attractive, friendly face into a sorrowful expression. "Forgive me for being so direct, but Tristan really is a monster—a cheater to the core."

"And who is this woman he's seeing behind Julia's back?" asked Victoria bluntly.

"Who? Oh, his secretary, Bianca Fleming."

"That's almost classic," Victoria commented, though she quirked the corners of her mouth sympathetically.

"You said it. He really doesn't miss a trick."

"And is Mr. Harrington perhaps also prone to violence?" Victoria pressed further, again very directly.

"Excuse me?"

"Well, the private detective who was watching him is dead now, isn't he?"

"You mean—? Well, no, I really can't imagine that. Tristan is a womanizer, sure, but hopefully not a murderer."

"*Hopefully* or definitely not?"

"Really, you are asking a lot of questions, Victoria..."

"I'm sorry. I'm just trying to help solve this murder, that's all. And as you said yourself, I don't want Mrs. Trapp to come to any harm—or anyone else, either. One murder victim is more than enough."

"Yes, of course. But honestly, Tristan as a murderer? No, it's definitely too far-fetched." He pushed away a pebble with the toe of his shoe, looking very thoughtful.

He wanted to take advantage of the brief awkward silence that had ensued to finally take his leave, but Victoria just kept talking regardless. "Forgive me for asking such an indiscreet question, but how is the marriage agreement between Mrs. Trapp and Mr. Harrington set out? In the event of divorce, or if Mrs. Trapp were to pass away? And does Mr. Harrington have any assets of his own?"

"We've trained Victoria quite well as an assistant detective so far, don't you think?" commented Pearl approvingly. "She almost sounds like a professional."

I groaned inwardly. Of course Pearl was right; Victoria had come to understand how to actively support us in our murder cases, even if in her eyes she was helping the inspector. She was somehow aware that Pearl and I were in fact solving the cases, but she usually explained our success away as being down to our instincts, or luck, coincidence or something of that sort. The fact that she was housing two four-pawed master sleuths under her roof just didn't fit into her human worldview.

But so be it—back to our current investigation. Victoria had just asked about the marital arrangements between Julia and Tristan, and so André readily provided her with the information she'd requested. I had the impression that it was doing him good to get his worries over Julia, to whom he was obviously very attached, off his chest for once.

"It's Julia who owns all the assets," he explained. "Her husband has only the modest income from the travel blog he runs. He's a bit of a big lifestyle influencer on Instagram and Facebook, you know. That's how he can spend a lot of time in the nicest hotels, but he doesn't necessarily get generous payouts on top of that. With his lavish lifestyle, he definitely relies on Julia's generosity. His father is a multimillionaire, of course, but he's still really spry and keeps his two sons pretty short financially, or so it seems to me. How Steven Harrington has settled his estate, I don't know, but Tristan can't expect an inheritance anytime soon, I should think."

"And what about a possible divorce between Julia and Tristan?" probed Victoria. "How would he fare financially then?"

"Well—there Tristan would go away empty-handed, whereas he would be the sole heir in the event of her death. There's a prenuptial contract that governs all of that. But you don't think he would do anything to Julia just because it would be financially advantageous for him?"

"Forgive me, I may be a little paranoid," Victoria said. "I've seen too many times that—oh, forget it."

"Okay..." André said nothing more, but he looked at Victoria quite worriedly, I thought.

I assumed, now that she was finally finished with her questions, that he would immediately return to Julia.

But he suddenly hesitated, standing there indecisively, kicked another pebble off the path and seemed to have something else on his mind.

Victoria noticed it, too, of course. "There's something else that's worrying you, isn't there?" she asked gently.

His chuckle seemed harsh to me. "You really are a good psychologist, Dr. Adler."

"Oh please, call me Victoria. That's quite enough formality, honestly. And thank you for the compliment."

"So Victoria—it's Julia I'm worried about. I don't know what's going on with her. Her moods ... no, that's not quite it. She's really not the stereotypical spoiled actress who annoys everyone around her with her changeable temperament. Quite the opposite, in fact. But she is—she was already, even before the private eye came to see us and informed her of her husband's infidelity—in kind of a strange mood. Depressed. Anxious? I don't know. She's otherwise such a positive, life-affirming person, despite her limited mobility. She loves her work ... and Tristan, though he hardly deserves it."

He frowned. "I guess when you fall in love with someone twice it's just fate, isn't it?"

"Twice?" Victoria repeated, uncomprehendingly. "Were they separated in between?"

"What? Oh no..." The nurse suddenly looked embarrassed. He glanced at his wristwatch and smiled at her stiffly. "I really have to go now, so if you'll excuse me?"

And before Victoria could say another word he had already moved away from us, taking great strides.

8

"We need to spy on Julia and her family some more," Pearl decided. "There's something topsy-turvy about them, most definitely. They must have a few skeletons in the closet, as they say."

"It seems like it to me, too. We'll have to sniff around this Tristan in person—and his secretary, with whom he's having the affair, as well. Julia is afraid, even if we don't know what is scaring her so much, and André still hasn't told us everything yet. Then there's also this strange boy who's been creeping around the house—he's also been hanging around the murder scene. So whose child is he? The dead detective's? Julia's? Or both of theirs together, maybe? No, that's crazy," I immediately contradicted myself.

"Hmm, maybe that's not so far-fetched. He could be a secret illegitimate child," Pearl opined. What if his parents aren't Julia and the detective? The boy could be from a previous affair of Tristan's, if he really is such a notorious womanizer. And he's cleverly concealing the little one from his wife—that's why the boy has to hide."

"But he'd hardly be hiding in the same house where she lives—let alone her vacation home. You watch too many soap operas on TV, Tiny," I remarked dryly.

"Pfft! That's not true at all. You know as well as I do

that I almost exclusively watch crime procedurals and thrillers. Soap operas are for Victoria."

"Yeah, but a lot of your favorite crime shows are also soap operas, in case you haven't noticed. Everything is always so super dramatic, and things happen that..." I hesitated.

Which would never happen in real life, I had been about to say. But considering everything that had taken place so far in our day to day lives, the remark was probably rather inappropriate. We were constantly met with murderers who killed their contemporaries for the craziest of motives. Our life *was* a soap opera.

"I certainly don't think a husband or wife could keep a child a secret from their spouse, especially in the same house," I finally said. "That would never work. And if Tristan had fathered offspring with a mistress, why would it live with *him*? It doesn't make any sense at all."

Pearl let the matter rest. Perhaps for once she saw that I was right.

"We have to make it clear to Victoria that we want to return to the villa. Inconspicuously—that is, without her," I said.

"Yes, let's do it like before," Pearl suggested. "I'll run toward the house and you stop her here, then you catch up to me."

"This time we have to scratch or bark at the door to get someone to open it for us. We can't wait around for some hotel employee to show up again to give us an entrance."

"Still, I'm sure it'll work out," Pearl said confidently.

"You think Julia or her caregiver will let us back into the house? What are they going to think? That Victoria keeps losing her pets, willy nilly?"

"Well, we can't worry about Victoria's image right now," Pearl replied. "We have a murder to solve!"

She was already toddling away. I hesitated for a moment, then stepped into Victoria's path and barked at her, just like I had done before when we had sneaked into Julia's vacation villa on our own for the first time.

But now Victoria understood almost immediately what we were up to. However, she decided that she should be in on it.

"You want to go back to the house?" she asked me. "Yeah, I guess that makes sense. The detective's death has something to do with this family, I could swear. I just need to find an excuse as to why I'm showing up on their doorstep again so soon. I imagine Julia and André don't feel like answering any more questions."

"That's why you have to stay here," I explained, pacing back and forth in front of her legs, continuing to block her path. "Pearl and I will spy on them. We can do it much better than you can—and without asking any questions."

She seemed to grasp what I was trying to tell her, but at the same time probably couldn't comprehend that Pearl and I were going to investigate by ourselves.

"Really now, Victoria," I complained with an emphatic yelp. "By now you should have realized that we're detectives. How many more murder cases do we have to solve before we get that through your head?"

She looked at me with wide eyes, and seemed to have no words to give me an answer. Finally she accompanied me toward the house anyway, as much as I jumped up and down in front of her to try to scare her away. However, I had to be careful not to bring her down.

I earned a critical look from Pearl, who was already sitting on the front step waiting for me when I showed up at the villa's door with Victoria in tow.

Before I could defend myself from Pearl's scorn, our two-legged had already rung the doorbell.

We had to wait only a few moments before it was opened and André welcomed us.

He first looked at Victoria in amazement.

She cleared her throat sheepishly, then she said, "Would it perhaps be possible for me to leave my pets with you for a while?

"The inspector needs my help," she lied, "probably for a few more hours. I would be able to pick them up again in the evening, if that suits? Athos and Pearl seem to have taken Julia very much to their hearts, and I think the reverse is also true. So would you mind, um, babysitting them for a bit?"

Pearl's little pink nose twitched. "Did she just say *babysit*?"

"It doesn't matter," I placated her, "the main thing is that we get into the house. I don't think her pretext is bad at all—and she did understand that we want to investigate alone. That's progress, Tiny!"

"But I don't want to be compared to *babies!*" she protested. "They're goofy, helpless, make a lot of noise, and usually don't smell very good."

For the life of me I didn't know the answer to that.

Fortunately, André immediately agreed to accommodate us for a while longer. He opened the door a bit further and Pearl marched straight past him. I followed her, while Victoria thanked him and said goodbye.

Pearl took a direct route to the kitchen. "So before we investigate any further now, I really need a snack. No ifs, ands, or buts this time. Before I actually starve to death."

However, André did not follow her, but disappeared in the direction of the living room. Pearl stopped, whirled around and meowed indignantly after him.

He halted and gave us a friendly look over his shoulder. "Well come on, you two, and keep us company in the living room. Julia will be so happy to see you, and you'll meet the rest of the family later, too. I'm sure they'll be surprised—after all, it's not every day we have four-pawed guests. Tristan's father is here, and his brother Jude, and their partners. They live in the house next door, you see, but now they've all come over and we're going to have dinner soon. To which you're both invited, of course."

He grinned. "I'm going to call room service again right now and see what delicious goodies they can supply for you guys."

"Fried fish would be nice," Pearl meowed back at him

in all seriousness, as if she were a high society lady placing her order at a gourmet restaurant.

Too bad for the tiny one that André didn't understand a word of what she'd said.

"At least you won't starve," I said. "Look on the bright side—you just have to be a little patient."

"Yes, yes, all right," the tiny one grumbled. "I'll just have to make a sacrifice. We must take advantage of the fact that the whole family has come together here today. We'll finally get to meet the others. I wonder if the secretary Tristan is cheating with is invited to dinner, too."

"I don't know. Let's go see."

9

We followed André into the living room.

However, we found only Julia sitting there, listlessly leafing through a women's magazine. André gave her a brief explanation of why we'd returned, and a small smile flitted across her lips. Otherwise, she looked rather gloomy and very thoughtful.

"Do you need me?" André asked her, and when she confirmed that "everything was perfect," he nodded politely and left the room.

"I think we should take a quick look around the house," I said to Pearl. "There's nothing going on in here right now."

She agreed with me, and so we set off to explore the villa's other rooms. Up till now we had hardly seen anything of this building, which was downright huge for holiday accommodation.

Julia didn't seem thrilled that we were leaving her again as soon as we'd arrived. "Where are you going?" she called, but fortunately she didn't follow after us.

Throughout the house we saw the same expensive-looking hardwood floors laid out as in the foyer, and I was careful not to damage any more of the floorboards with my claws. Paintings and photographs hung cheerily on the walls, the colors of the furnishings were bright and inviting throughout, and the style was more modern than the houses appeared to be from the outside.

In the dining room, where hopefully dinner would soon be served to keep my little glutton from starving, we found Tristan's brother and his wife. They were a completely mismatched couple. He was a lean, plainly dressed man, who looked as if he had never taken a risk or had an adventure in his life. He wore a three-piece suit even though he was on vacation, and had short dark hair of the rough-haired dachshund type.

His wife, on the other hand, was what people call a beauty: tall, slender, with the fine golden-blonde hair of a Saluki and plenty of color on her face. Her lips were made up in a dark red lipstick, her eyes framed in dazzling shades of blue, and she wore a skimpy, garishly colored dress that clung to her body like a second skin. She was also wearing a fruity perfume that smelled very exotic.

We only learned their names because they addressed each other by them—or rather, they nagged at each other.

"You're such a zero, Jude!"

"And you're a terrible bitch, my dear Celeste."

And so on.

They didn't introduce themselves to us, of course, as hardly any humans do when an animal enters the room. They did give us both a brief, astonished look, but then they continued with the activity they'd been engrossed in when we'd appeared: they carried on arguing.

First of all, they quarreled about the fact that Celeste had dreamed of a somewhat sunnier vacation spot than a winter stay on Sylt.

"What are we doing here, in this wasteland?" she grumbled. "Why didn't we fly to the Maldives like you've been promising me for so long?"

Jude scowled at her. "Father just bought this hotel, and he wanted to celebrate his birthday here. We couldn't miss it. It's only logical, don't you think?"

"Your father, always your father! And what about me—what about my wishes and my needs?"

"Oh please, honey..."

"I mean it. You let him order you around and take advantage of you like some kind of personal servant. This has got to stop, damn it! You slave away for him around the clock, you're practically his right-hand man, and yet he pays you like a private secretary. No, an errand boy!"

"He's just stingy—he always has been."

"Are you trying to defend him too, or what? You have to stand up for your own interests for once, Jude! For *our* interests. We can't go on living like this forever."

"What's so bad about the way we live?"

Celeste wrinkled her nose the way Pearl does when a piece of common sausage is put in front of her. "You're not seriously asking me that, are you? You're such a wuss. I could puke!"

"Celeste really, you're going too far! You mustn't talk to me like that." His words sounded quite pitiful. Unfortunately it had to be said that he did not stand up for himself to her, either.

Celeste, whose cheeks were now glowing red, went on: "Your father is one of the richest men I know, while we live like the petit bourgeois. You have to talk to him, Jude, promise me! After dinner is a good time—over a nice glass of sherry. The old man likes it so much, after all. Tell him plainly that a raise is long overdue—and don't let him try to fob you off with a tip, do you hear?"

Jude admitted defeat, nodding dutifully. I couldn't tell who made him more afraid, his father or his ultra-demanding wife. The poor man was really not to be envied.

We found Julia's husband Tristan in a small study upstairs, and his secretary Bianca—with whom he was having the affair, according to Edward Laymon's research—was with him.

However, to my surprise the two of them weren't actually canoodling, but were apparently working hard. Both were sitting behind open laptops and discussing a feature article and photo spread focusing on Steven Harrington's new hotel resort here on Sylt.

Tristan was a very handsome man, although as a dog I'm not too much of an expert on these things. He definitely resembled Jude, but was sort of the glossy, premium version of his brother. He was also dark-haired, but his locks fell in boldly styled waves down his face and he wore fashionable sportswear. He was much more powerfully built than his brother was, appearing confident and very pleased with himself.

Bianca was dressed rather strictly, in a tight skirt, white blouse and gray jacket. She smelled of coconut, probably due to her shampoo or shower gel, and had long, light brown hair. She seemed to be concentrating intensely on her work, so that she glanced at Pearl and me only briefly, asked in surprise who we belonged to, and then immediately continued typing away on her laptop.

Tristan at least took the time to pat my head and make a delighted sound over Pearl.

"I don't know where Julia got these two," he said. "What a mismatched pair! My wife is a real animal lover, you know. I hope she hasn't adopted them permanently. I mean, the kitten is adorable, but this husky is clearly too bulky to be an appropriate pet—most unsuitable."

He smiled. "Although of course, Julia wouldn't give a moment's thought to such a thing. When she wants something she doesn't care how impractical others might find it."

Bianca just nodded and continued with her typing.

I was angry about the eternal confusion of my Malamute self with a husky, and that Tristan had called me *bulky*, but I didn't let on. Unfortunately I've had to become used to such abuse.

Not that I have anything against huskies, of course, but they are not half so imposing as we Malamutes are—sort of like house cats compared to lions.

Was Pearl's vanity slowly starting to rub off on me, that I was worrying about such things?

Hopefully not.

Tristan and Bianca returned to the conversation they'd been having when we showed up. They discussed the hotel feature spread, which apparently would be ready soon, and Bianca noted down her boss's ideas on her computer, but also added minor notes of her own.

Tristan gestured animatedly with his hands, and leaned over to Bianca gradually more and more as he talked. As if by chance his fingers would brush her arms or shoulders—and my nose caught that unmistakable scent that people emit when they find a member of the opposite sex attractive. Both Bianca and Tristan smelled very aroused.

This, of course, came as no surprise to me. After all, according to Edward Laymon, the two had quite the adulterous relationship going, even if they apparently didn't resort to kissing or groping at work. Really disciplined, one had to say.

10

Pearl and I continued our pilgrimage through the house, exploring all the rooms while tracking down Tristan's father, Steven, and his partner.

They had settled into a smaller living room upstairs, and were as surprised to see the two of us as Tristan and Bianca had been earlier.

Steven was an older man, as to be expected of someone with two middle-aged sons, but his girlfriend, whose name was Scarlett, must have been at least thirty years his junior.

Unlike Tristan and Bianca, these two were flirting quite openly. Scarlett was sitting on the sofa next to Steven with her arm around his shoulders, and was just talking about how beautiful she thought the hotel was when we arrived. "It's a dreamy place," she cooed. "Let's stay here a while longer, honey."

He nodded in agreement. "In any case, at least until Christmas. I must say that I love the winter here on Sylt. I wouldn't have thought so, but still, there it is. And by the way, dear, I will soon have more free time. Just like you always wished for—then we'll be able to spend a lot more time traveling."

"More free time? What do you mean by that?" asked Scarlett in amazement.

"You'll see, sweetie. Allow me to surprise you."

When we returned to the living room a short while later, Julia had moved from her wheelchair to the couch and was reading a book. Judging from the picture on the cover, it was a romance novel.

"Hmm, not much action happening here," Pearl complained.

"What did you expect—that we'd witness the family members openly killing each other off?"

"That would speed things up, wouldn't it?" said the pipsqueak. "Then we could solve the murder case in record time for once. On the other hand, it might be kind of boring."

"Mail for you, Mrs. Trapp," a voice suddenly said behind us. Bianca had entered the room. She had an envelope with her which she handed to Julia. She looked very nervous as she did so.

Julia looked at her as if she were facing a poisonous reptile in the wild. "A letter? Who delivered it?" she asked in a sharp tone. She stared at the typed letters on the envelope, which presumably formed her name. Unfortunately I still have a problem with reading human writing.

"I don't know," Bianca replied uncertainly. "It must have been pushed under the front door, because I just found it in the hallway on the floor. It had your name on it, so I thought I'd drop it off."

She handed the letter to Julia and was already turning to leave.

"Wait," the actress said sharply. "I wanted to talk to you."

My fine nose caught the instant Bianca began to sweat.

"Yes?" she asked timidly.

"Oh, don't pretend to be so clueless," Julia snapped. "You know exactly what this is about—my husband, whom you are trying to fish for. No, whom you've already hooked, you little tramp! Don't think I'm going to give him up that easily." Julia leaned forward and glared angrily at the secretary. "I want your resignation, do you hear me? And I want it now."

"You're wrong," Bianca managed, her face suddenly chalk white. "There's nothing going on between Mr. Harrington and me. I just work for him, that's all."

Julia clicked her tongue. If she'd had whiskers like Pearl, they would have vibrated and twitched wildly with anger.

"Oh, please,"—she practically spat it in Bianca's face—"do you honestly believe I'm going to buy your load of bullshit? I've worked with the best actresses in the world; do you really think you can wrap me around your little finger, with the little song and dance you're putting on? I have it in black and white what a lecherous little beast you are, and how skillfully you have gotten close to my husband and seduced him. I am in possession of plenty of photographic proof that leaves nothing to the imagination. And the man who took them is now dead."

"But..." Bianca stammered.

Julia grinned with sour satisfaction. "You're looking smart there, huh? Like a deer caught in headlights. Really, a great performance—village pantomime level, but still." Her beautiful face contorted into a hateful snarl. "Get the hell out of here! Out of Tristan's office, and out of his life. Do you understand me?"

Bianca said nothing in reply. I could tell she was fighting back tears. Her lower lip quivered, although she pushed her jaw forward defiantly. She wanted to fight back, it seemed to me, but was paralyzed in the face of her competitor's undisguised hostility.

She stood motionless for another brief moment, then hurried out of the room as if the devil were after her.

11

We slipped out of the room behind Bianca, of course leaving enough of a distance after her that she didn't feel followed. But she had disappeared into one of the rooms on the ground floor—probably her bedroom?—and slammed the door behind her.

Pearl and I looked at each other. We heard quiet sobbing, then the next moment an angry scream. Bianca was giving free rein to her frustration now that she thought herself unobserved. Then something smashed against the wall in the room, which judging by the crash had shattered into a thousand pieces, and Bianca uttered a nasty curse that I won't repeat here. Let's just say that she wished the plague and worse upon Julia.

Pearl and I paused outside the door for a moment, but when there was nothing more to be heard we trotted back toward the dining room.

Both of us were cherishing the hope that dinner would soon be served. I was definitely feeling quite hungry; owing to all our snooping we had not had a proper meal all day. The detective's life is a hard one indeed!

But as we crept along the unlit corridor, I suddenly heard a noise—the pattering of tiny feet. I pricked up my ears and twisted my head back and forth to find out from which direction it came.

"Up ahead, over there," I heard Pearl say.

She sped up and ran down the hall, and I saw a shadow disappear from the darkness of the hallway into a room a few dog lengths ahead of us. The door moved ever so slightly; someone small and slender must have slipped through.

"That's Julia's bedroom," Pearl said softly to me. She was already trying to squeeze through the crack in the door behind the shadow.

"Stay here with me!" I protested. "You're not going in there by yourself! It's way too dangerous! Let's take a look first and see who that shadow is."

She listened to me for once, and so we just silently and carefully stuck our muzzles through the crack in the door, hers below and mine above her.

At first glance the room looked deserted. None of the lamps were lit, and only some moonlight was falling into the room through the windows. Darkness had come hours ago on this dull November evening up here in the north.

And then we saw him: the strange little boy who had now crossed our path for the third time. He was standing in front of Julia's bedside table, which he overtopped by just a paw's width, and seemed to be examining two objects that were laid out there.

"A bowl, just like that one in the kitchen this afternoon—and a bottle," Pearl said, her sharp cat's eyes seeing better in the darkness than I could, "with ... hmm, oranges on the label, as far as I can tell. It must be orange juice. It's Julia's favorite drink, apparently. She had a bottle within reach over in the living room, too."

"Well done," I praised her, "but what is the boy doing here? And—oh!" I almost howled in shock.

With a sweeping movement of his hand, the little two-legged had thrown the bottle of orange juice off the nightstand. It broke on the floor with a clink.

I couldn't help thinking of Pearl when she was bored. It was then that she loved to run around on shelves or on chests of drawers and tables and throw things down. Fascinated, she'd watch the objects fall and break, like a little scientist.

Just the other day when Pearl had destroyed a vase in this way, and Victoria had rushed in because of the noise, I was blessed with a demonstration of the tiny one's amazing acting ability. Pearl had managed to dramatically drop to the floor next to the broken pieces just as Victoria had rushed into the room. And our kind-hearted two-legged had actually thought the poor kitten had fallen, breaking the vase in the process.

What a palaver! Pearl might be a lazy, gluttonous and pampered sofa-loving cat, but she could clamber around on the furniture like a little monkey. And if she overestimated her leaps, she always landed softly and quite unharmed on her velveteen paws.

The little boy with the pointed cap seemed to have a similar disposition to Madame Cat in this sense. He stood motionless and stared at the floor, seemingly fascinated. He was probably looking at the broken pieces of glass, or watching the orange juice spread across the floorboards. The mess seemed to delight him.

He turned his head briefly and waited. Apparently he wanted to know if someone had heard the clink.

But no one appeared. Pearl and I remained motionless in the doorway, fading into the darkness and not even daring to breathe.

In the next moment, the boy grabbed the bowl of cereal from off the nightstand.

I thought it would meet the same tragic fate as the bottle, but instead of sweeping it off the nightstand, the boy seized it in one of his bony hands and pressed it to his chest like some sort of treasure. Then he climbed with it onto the bed and settled cross-legged on the pillow. He put his index finger into the bowl and the very next moment he was licking it with relish.

I could not believe my eyes.

"He must be Julia's child," I heard Pearl's voice saying—so softly that at first I didn't know if I was just hallucinating.

Not a far-fetched assumption, given what was happening here, right before my eyes. Perhaps the porridge had been intended for the boy, and Julia had left the bowl here for him to find?

"He's waiting for his mother in her bedroom," said the tiny one, "but why is he eating here alone, away from the others? Do you think Julia is hiding the little one because he is a bit strange? But she herself is in a wheelchair—surely she can't be one of those two-leggeds who reject others purely on the basis that they're not quite normal?"

"It looks that way," I said. "And to rebel against such poor treatment, the little guy throws things on the floor. By the way, we didn't see toys anywhere in the house. Did you notice that?"

"We should have a talk with the kid," Pearl said. "I'll go first. You might scare him."

Already she was toddling off. I didn't hold her back, because although the child might behave strangely he didn't really look dangerous. He would not strangle my tiny one with his bare hands. I couldn't always smother Pearl like a concerned mother hen!

Pearl put up her tail and tripped toward the boy with a soft meow. It meant something like, "Hey kid, what's up?"

And what did he do? He leaped up from the bed as if bitten by a wild monkey, maneuvered the bowl back onto the nightstand, and before I knew what was happening he had disappeared under the bed before my very eyes.

I ran into the room, barked once, then threw myself on my stomach and peered under the bedstead. But it was so dark there that I couldn't see a thing.

"Little boy?" called Pearl. "Are you there? You don't have to hide from us—we won't hurt you."

But the child did not so much as let out a peep.

I pushed myself closer to the bed, while Pearl was

already crawling into the crack which had swallowed the boy.

I heard her sneeze. Then, "He's not here. There's only dust down here."

I heard a noise to my left. I quickly turned my head and imagined that I could make out a shadow flitting through the gap in the doorway and out into the hall. However, I was not quite sure.

What kind of strange boy *was* this? No human I had ever met was so nimble and so silent on his feet. But a ghost, on the other hand, certainly did not eat porridge. Were Pearl and I suffering from delusions—and did the boy exist only in our overheated imaginations?

Victoria had said that shared hallucinations are extremely rare, and animals are not as neurotic as humans. We usually don't see anything that doesn't exist.

The fur on the back of my neck bristled. Something was not quite right in this hotel. What kind of mess had we gotten ourselves into this time?

Pearl appeared next to me and sneezed again. "Why did that little runt take off? Who on earth is afraid of a cute kitten?" she asked indignantly.

12

At dinner, Pearl had to suffer a bitter disappointment. The hotel kitchen served a variety of delicacies, but none of the two-leggeds present had chosen fish. In addition to this, André had forgotten to fulfill his promise and order something for us to eat. Therefore he descended in Pearl's esteem from the status of "quite nice" to "the worst of animal abusers." To make matters worse, Scarlett was firmly of the opinion that feeding animals from the table was a bad habit.

"You mustn't do it under any circumstances," she instructed the other two-leggeds, "otherwise they will beg constantly and at every meal. The owner of these two will definitely not appreciate that."

To cut a long story short, Pearl and I didn't get a single delicious morsel from the table, but went entirely empty-pawed.

Pearl turned her back on the humans and dropped onto her belly—ostensibly totally exhausted and on the verge of starvation. She put her muzzle on my front paw and pouted.

After their meal, however, the humans again attracted our attention, even though we would have preferred to have further ignored them. Another set of waiters emerged from the main hotel, bringing desserts, coffee, and some foul-smelling spirits. When they'd disappeared again, Steven Harrington pinged his dessert spoon against a glass and announced that he had something important to tell us.

Pearl didn't move from her spot, but I could see her little ears twitching. She was listening closely, just like me.

"You all know I'm celebrating my seventieth in a few weeks," Steven began in a serious tone, belied by the smile on his face, as if he took great pleasure in what he was about to reveal.

He looked to me like the typical family man about to hand out prettily-wrapped Christmas presents beneath a bauble-bedecked fir tree. And yet there was something wrong with this cozy picture—something mischievous, perhaps even evil, sparkled in his eyes.

But no, I was surely just imagining it. It was obvious I had already met too many sneaky two-leggeds for one dog's lifetime.

"But you're still going strong, Father," Jude joked.

Tristan joined in: "Right, here's to another thirty years, I say!" He raised his glass. "At least!"

"Sweet of you boys—I do hope to reach my hundred," Steven said good-humoredly, "but come what may, I certainly don't intend to spend the late fall and winter of my life behind a desk. And that's precisely why I've decided to retire. I want to enjoy the fruits of my decades of labor before I—oh, you know—jump in the box."

"What?" gasped Tristan. "But you're in the middle of the most amazing success story, you've just bought this wonderful hotel here, and—"

Steven silenced him with an imperious wave of his hand. "It's a done deal, son," he said. "What I'm concerned with now is finding my optimal successor, who will lead Harrington Hotels into the future—and indeed expand it even further."

He looked first at Jude, then at Tristan. "I want one of you two to take over my company. The other—"

"Expand even further?" Julia interrupted, apparently without really thinking first about the effect her words might have. "You already own a hotel in every one-horse town in the world."

She received a withering look from Steven and an equally venomous one from Tristan, at which she visibly flinched.

His father's announcement had probably come as a surprise to everyone, but Tristan had obviously made up his mind within seconds that he wanted to outdo his brother and be made the heir to the hotel empire. That would certainly make him a massively wealthy man, who would no longer be dependent on his wife's money.

Julia's sarcastic remark about the hotel chain, however, could hardly have helped her husband's chances in his father's eyes.

She backpedaled, muttering, "Sorry, Steven, I was just kidding. Your hotel chain is amazing, and the resort here on Sylt is ... the cherry on the cake. It, um, really has a very special flair."

Steven nodded at her, his expression mollified,

which probably meant that he had graciously forgiven her for once.

Then he turned back to his two sons and set out his plan in detail. "You have two weeks to convince me as to which of you I should choose as my ideal successor. The other will receive a one-time payment of one million euros, so your livelihood will be secured—that is important to me as your father—but then don't expect a generous inheritance when I die. I intend to spend it all in the next few years ... or decades perhaps, if I have that much time left. I want to live like a king and die a poor man. After all, you can't fill your coffin with gold."

He chuckled and looked around as if he had made a particularly amusing joke.

Both Tristan and Jude seemed most put out. So they were supposed to compete against each other in some kind of contest—a tournament between brothers with a really fat prize at stake.

The one million euros that the loser was to receive sounded quite impressive, but compared to the value of the Harrington hotel chain it was surely a mere gratuity.

The ins and outs of the two-leggeds' financial dealings weren't really my thing, but I'd lived among them long enough to know all the things they were willing to do for money. Sometimes the most outrageous things. And a million euros was a lot of brass. Quite a lot of dough. Or bread. A huge pile of moolah. Lots and lots of ducats. Or scratch. Bucks, coin, bob, pence. The humans called their beloved money by the most outlandish names.

We dogs are much more logical—a steak is a steak, a bone is a bone. We don't use strange expressions for what is important to us. It's a wonder that the two-leggeds rule the world and not us, but still it's better than if the cats were in charge!

Back to Steven and his announcement: it didn't escape me that Bianca looked positively impressed by the patriarch's words. Scarlett, on the other hand, was sitting there with a face like thunder, looking as if she wanted to jump down Steven's throat.

In the grandiose announcement of his plans for the future, he had not mentioned her, his own partner, with a single word. What was he going to leave *her*? Was she to go away empty-handed when it came to the division of his considerable fortune? At his death, she would probably inherit nothing, if indeed he intended to squander everything as he had said.

13

The gathering in the dining room duly broke up, with most of those present wordlessly leaving the room. Pearl and I got up onto our paws, and I stretched and tried to ignore the grumbling of my stomach, which was getting quite loud.

André prepared to push Julia out of the room in her wheelchair behind the others. Apart from Steven, the two of them were the last ones in the room.

But the old man raised his voice to forestall her exit. "Why don't you keep me company a little longer, Julia?"

He gave André a quick meaningful glance, and the latter took the not very subtle hint that he should move out of earshot.

The patriarch apparently hadn't noticed that Pearl and I were still in the room. In any case, he probably did not find us to be intruding. It really was invaluable that people allowed us pets to fade into the background like furniture instead of considering us the little spies that we truly were.

Steven waited until the door had closed behind the nurse-companion, then put on a sympathetic expression and asked Julia in a most grandfatherly voice, "My dear Julia, what's wrong with you? You seem so distressed. Don't you like my hotel?"

"What? Yes, of course," she replied quickly. "I thought I told you. It's just terrific." She sounded one hundred percent sincere.

The old man nodded, even as he looked into her eyes with an intense, piercing gaze.

Julia straightened her shoulders and rolled a little closer to him. She seemed to weigh what she wanted to say for a moment, but then she got to the point immediately. "You know, Steven, as far as your legacy is concerned—that is, the handing over of the hotel chain to your successor—Tristan is the more capable of your sons. A blind man could see that, couldn't he? So you should leave your resorts to him if you don't want your life's work to go down the drain."

Steven's upper lip curled. "That may be, but Jude has been a loyal son to me all these years, taking care of his father, while I've only seen your dear husband twice a year at best. Jude may not be a genius, but he is reliable ... a quality that is all too often underestimated. And he has an ambitious wife who would support him vigorously if I bequeathed him my hotel chain, I'm sure."

"Yes, I suppose that's true," Julia countered. "Celeste will do whatever it takes to get her hands on your legacy, and then she'll spend the company's assets hand over fist. Is that really what you want?"

Steven gave Julia a critical look that probably meant something like: *and how would you stand by Tristan if I made him the hotel heir?*

She did not answer directly, but only repeated what

she had already said: "You should bet on Tristan ... for your own sake."

A small pause arose, during which the two regarded each other like opponents facing off in a ring. Then Steven suddenly dropped his shoulders and said, "I'm tired. It's been a long day."

Julia accepted his cue. She grabbed the wheels of her chair and deftly maneuvered herself to the door and out of the room.

Pearl and I followed her, but she only drove as far as the bedroom her caregiver occupied, then stopped at the door and seemed to lose herself in thought instead of knocking.

The pipsqueak and I restlessly—and perhaps a little haphazardly—made a new circuit of the house. Was there something else we needed to explore? Another conversation to eavesdrop on between the humans that might finally give us a clue as to what exactly was going on in this family—and whether or not these people had had anything to do with the death of detective Edward Laymon?

We came to the living room and bumped into Bianca, who was having a drink with Scarlett—whiskey, if my nose didn't deceive me.

They weren't talking about murder, but still, Scarlett was in a miserable mood.

"Well, my dear, I hope tonight has taught you a lesson," she said to Bianca in a bitter tone. "It never pays to be your boss's mistress. You'll always remain just a bed toy to him, a fling that's truly meaningless. When it comes to making his big life plans, you don't even get a look-in!"

She took a big sip from her glass, and I could see the anger blazing in her eyes—and the mortification, besides. I also suspected that this wasn't the first drink she'd had since dinner, as her cheeks were flushed and she was downing the foul-smelling stuff so quickly that her glass would soon be empty.

"I'm not my boss's mistress," Bianca told her firmly.

"Oh? Now who are you kidding, my girl? I see the way you look at him—and how he looks at you. Aside from the fact that he's only going to break your heart, let me give you some good advice: watch out for Julia. Trust me, you don't want her as an enemy, and she'll never give up Tristan without a fight. She's crazy about him, in case you haven't noticed. No matter how many times he may have cheated on her."

"But I just told you that there's nothing going on between him and me—"

"Yeah, yeah, okay. I don't really care." She grimaced, then added, "Anyway, Tristan definitely has the hots for you. Take it from me."

Bianca abruptly changed the subject. She went on the attack instead of defending herself further. "You're disappointed that Steven didn't bother to include you in his succession plans, aren't you?" she said bluntly.

"Disappointed?" Scarlett snapped at her. "Pissed off is more like it! I sacrificed my life to that bastard, damn it. I did all the dirty work he was too good for, made him and his stupid hotel chain huge, helped him succeed. He'd be a nobody without me. And for my reward, I got to play second fiddle to his wife for years. Ha!"

She stared into her glass with a frustrated expression. Then she continued, "On the outside, it was always the perfect marriage. *Family above all else*, is Steven's motto. His wife was just so lazy and stupid, you know. Not like Celeste or Julia, they're both smart—they have brains. And they are both very assertive and independent. They know what they want. I bet those two will work it out between themselves as to who gets the hotel chain in the end."

"Don't speak ill of the dead, they say," Bianca opined.

"I know, but it's true! There's just nothing positive to say about Steven's late wife."

"So you and Steven ... were you together when she was alive?" asked Bianca.

Scarlett hesitated; then she drained her whiskey glass. "Yes, damn it, I was his mistress for years," she said. "What's the point of denying it now, to you of all people, when you're in the same boat?" She set her glass down on the tabletop with far too much momentum. It was a wonder it didn't break.

Bianca opened her mouth, perhaps to affirm once again that there was nothing going on between her and Tristan. But then apparently she changed her mind. "What did Steven's wife die of, anyway?" she asked instead. "She couldn't have been old, could she?"

"Nah, she was a scant ten years younger than him. Samantha was an avid hiker, and she never came back from a trip in the mountains."

"Oh, God, how awful. What happened?"

"I don't know. Her body was never found."

14

Our spy mission wasn't even close to being over, and by now I was not only hungry as a wolf but also tired to the bone. Pearl did not seem to have fared any better; she was taciturn and rose only sluggishly onto her paws when we prepared to leave the living room.

But an opportunity to observe another conversation still presented itself, and dutifully—for fear of missing something important—we seized upon it.

We followed Bianca, who'd left Scarlett alone in the living room, straight upstairs to the small chamber that she and Tristan used as a study. She was so lost in thought that she didn't even notice Pearl and me following her. Not even when we slipped into the study right behind her, just before she closed the door.

Tristan was sitting in front of his computer again, but abruptly stopped typing when we entered the room. He looked down at Pearl, smiled, and then patted his thighs with both hands. Probably an invitation to cuddle, but Pearl did not take him up on it. Her mood seemed to have hit rock bottom.

I honestly wondered why she hadn't been crying her eyes out to me about how she was going to die of hunger at any moment. It seemed she wanted to prove to me her bravery in detective work.

Tristan gave up his attempt to attract Pearl and

looked up. When he saw Bianca's serious face, he frowned.

"Are you all right?" he asked.

"I—I'm just a little tired," she said. "It's been a long day."

Pearl and I knew, of course, that this was far from the whole truth. Julia's wish—or should I say her demand?—that Bianca should quit her job as his secretary was clearly bothering her. There was no overlooking it, or indeed over-smelling it. The young woman reeked of stress, and even a bit of fear.

Tristan seemed to know her very well, because he didn't let himself be fooled. Instead he tried to question her.

"You look like you've seen a ghost," he said. "You know you can talk to me about anything, right? I may be your boss, but I'm also—I'd like to be—"

He stammered and finally clammed up. Then he looked at Bianca all the more intensely.

I expected that at any moment he would leap up and snatch her into his arms. After all, they were lovers, weren't they?

But that didn't happen; Bianca only sighed softly and dropped into the vacant chair that stood next to the desk. "Your wife thinks we're having an affair," she said.

"What? Oh God—where did you get that idea? Did she confront you with it?"

"Gave me hell is more like it," Bianca said. "She wants me to quit my job with you, or I'll be sorry, she says."

"Oh my goodness." He reached for her hand, but she withdrew it gently.

"I'm so sorry," he said in a raspy voice. "Julia can sometimes—" He made a helpless gesture, then ran both hands through his hair. "She tends to be jealous, I'm afraid."

"But she doesn't have the slightest reason for it," Bianca exclaimed. "I would never start anything with my boss, especially not if he were married."

"I know that," Tristan said. The look he gave Bianca, however, seemed to contain something like regret in the face of this declaration.

"What the heck?" Pearl exclaimed. "Is there really nothing going on between them?"

"Looks like it," I replied. "They're hardly going to put on a show just on our account, are they?"

"No, definitely not," the tiny one agreed. "They'd be the first two-leggeds to think of us as any kind of dangerous witnesses."

"But that detective took pictures of the two of them," I reminded Pearl, "in explicit situations. Or did we get something wrong?"

"We didn't," said the tiny one. "Julia more than hinted at it, even to Bianca—that she and Tristan were caught cheating, in the act. I don't suppose there was any talk of simply holding hands."

"I didn't get that impression either," I replied.

And almost as if Bianca had decided to confirm our conversation, she said to Tristan: "Your wife claimed that this detective who was murdered had photographs of us—making out and whatnot. Nah, worse than that. The way Julia attacked me, the photos must be of us in bed!"

"Excuse me?" Tristan gasped. His eyes snapped open. "But there's no such thing. It's not like we're ... we're not guilty of anything. Not a thing." There it was again, that look, as if he regretted it. As if he would be only too happy to go to bed with Bianca. As long as he wasn't caught by his wife or some detective, of course.

Tristan's body exuded a fierce cocktail of scents that told me he was exceedingly keen on his secretary.

"Anyway, your wife hired that detective to spy on us," Bianca said, "and now he's dead. I find it rather alarming, don't you?"

"Of course," Tristan said quickly. "Julia doesn't think we had anything to do with it, I hope? Heaven knows what she told that Chief Inspector. She can be terribly hot-headed sometimes."

"I've noticed that, too," Bianca mumbled to herself with a pinched expression on her face.

"Now what is that supposed to mean?" I said to Pearl, confused. "Did the detective lie to Julia about Tristan's infidelity?"

Pearl didn't have the opportunity to answer me, however, because Bianca drew our attention again with a sudden change of subject.

"I wanted to talk to you about your father's offer, Tristan," she said, already sounding more composed.

"The hotel chain?" he asked.

Bianca nodded, giving him a meaningful look. "I suppose you don't want to let your brother have it," she said, "or am I mistaken? If you could inherit your father's assets, even now in his lifetime, you wouldn't be financially dependent on your wife."

"Bianca..." His eyes suddenly lit up. "What are you getting at?" He lifted his hand and gently stroked her arm.

She smiled as mysteriously as a sphinx. "I think the Harrington hotels are gorgeous—not just this one here, but the others all around the world. I've already looked at a few on the website. Your father has really built something unique, put so much heart and soul into it, and there is so much potential, I think. I have a few ideas..."

She hesitated, and her face became serious again. Quite businesslike, in fact.

Then she said, "What would it be worth to you if I helped you beat Jude—if we could get your father to sign the hotels over to you? Would you let me have, say, ten percent of the shares? That would be appropriate, I should think, and a good deal for both of us. I feel we make an excellent team. We'd work fantastically together as partners, what do you think?"

"But how on earth ... are you going to do that?" asked Tristan in surprise. "Beat Jude? What do you have in mind?"

"Just leave it all to me," Bianca said. "Can we put a written agreement together? Ten percent for me if you get the hotel chain signed over to you."

Tristan looked rather shocked. He was silent for a moment, seeming to be considering the offer. But then he nodded slowly.

15

"What can Bianca be up to?" Pearl asked me. "How is she going to outsmart Jude and get Steven to bequeath his hotels to Tristan?"

But to this, of course, I had no answer.

We trotted back to the living room again, where we now found Julia surfing the internet on her cell phone. She immediately put it away when we came in so she could play a bit with Pearl.

Both the pipsqueak and I were at a loss concerning what to do next. There were plenty of secrets here, bad blood and perhaps sinister intentions among these two-leggeds, but that one of them had murdered the detective—we'd found no proof of that.

It wasn't long before Victoria showed up with Oskar in tow. André came into the room with the two of them, although their arrival had been announced to us earlier by the ringing of the doorbell.

"Thank you for watching my little ones," Victoria said to Julia as the Chief Inspector asked to be seated for a moment.

"I have news for you, Mrs. Trapp, regarding the murder of your private detective," he announced.

"You were able to catch the perpetrator?" Julia asked hopefully.

Oskar frowned in response. "Not yet, unfortunately.

But in our research on Edward Laymon, we came across—how shall I put it? A detail I don't want to keep from you. An inconsistency that has puzzled me exceedingly."

"Yes—what is it? Please don't keep me in suspense."

"Well," said Oskar, "it turns out that Edward Laymon was not a private detective at all, and neither was he an ex-policeman, bodyguard, mercenary, or anyone else who could do confidential investigations for pay. Rather he was a petty criminal, who already had several cases on file with us. The man had half a dozen prior convictions: minor offenses, theft, drug possession.... But he was not, to our knowledge, violent."

"I beg your pardon?" Julia said sharply. "It can't be. You must be mistaken."

"No, it is a certainty, trust me. I have personally verified all the information that is available about him," the Chief Inspector affirmed. "Which now brings me to the question of how you originally became aware of Mr. Laymon's services—did he approach you and offer himself as a private detective? Or how did you come to know of him?"

Before Julia could answer, André inserted himself into the conversation.

"Mrs. Trapp hired Mr. Laymon on my recommendation," he said with a contrite expression. "Edward was an old school friend of mine, Chief Inspector. That is, *friend* is probably saying too much," he qualified. "We knew each other fairly well in our youth, but that was some fifteen years ago now. After we graduated we lost track of each other, but then a few months ago we got together again at a class reunion—and that's when he told me that he was working as a private detective. I didn't question it, of course; it would never have occurred to me that he was lying. What you've just said, that he was a criminal, had committed thefts and was involved with drugs..."

He shook his head with a startled expression. "I don't know the first thing about that.... I knew him as an upright fellow, with both feet firmly on the right path in life. And on the right side of the law! He didn't smoke or drink, and he honestly didn't come across as a junkie, let alone a drug dealer. I just don't believe it."

"People can change, Mr. Meissner," the Chief Inspector said. "Sometimes not for the better, unfortunately."

"Looks like it," André said. "Poor Edward—I wonder what happened to him in life to bring him to this, to make him go completely off the rails?"

"I really don't know, I'm sorry," said Oskar.

"Yes, of course. But anyway.... Um, when Julia was looking for a private investigator, I immediately thought of Edward. As I've said, I thought he was quite trustworthy, and so I called him, and he agreed to take on the job. I had no idea that he was—oh my God, what was he actually doing? Why was he posing as a private detective? Was it some scam he was running to get rich?"

"He did fulfill my request, though," Julia interjected before Oskar could reply. "He gave me the information I paid him to acquire and I had no reason to complain.

Please don't blame yourself, André," she said, turning to her nurse. "You couldn't have known he was lying to you about his credentials. It's not like you go and do a background check first before you hire a private investigator. That would be absurd."

"You're right about that," the Chief Inspector said.

Neither he nor Julia went into more detail regarding the reason she had originally hired Edward Laymon. So much for researching an applicant for a position she wanted to fill, as she had claimed to the Chief Inspector at the beginning....

Pearl and I knew better, of course, and I assumed that Victoria had also already passed on to the detective what she had earlier learned from André in private—namely, that Julia hired the detective in order to put her husband under surveillance. In any case, the Chief Inspector did not ask her any more questions concerning the exact nature of Edward Laymon's assignment here on Sylt.

"It makes sense, I think," Pearl murmured to me. "This so-called detective being no sleuth at all but rather a criminal ... he lied to Julia about Tristan and Bianca having an affair, didn't he? The two of them don't actually have a relationship."

"It looks like it, yes," I said. "But that would also mean that Laymon must have faked the photos he presented to Julia. The humans have the right computer programs for that, don't they? But what's the point of it exactly? And does his death have anything to do with his fraud?"

"Maybe he just wanted to provide Julia with the results she expected," Pearl suggested. "To give himself the veneer of being a professional detective."

"Yes—and what for? Just to collect his fee?" I had to object.

"It's possible," the pipsqueak said. "Perhaps he thought it better than actually stealing."

"I have another idea," I said. "What if he wanted to blackmail Tristan with those faked photos—or even Bianca?"

"Tristan isn't rich enough to make it worthwhile, though," Pearl replied. "His wife has all the money, not him."

"Maybe Laymon didn't know that," I argued. "To the outside world, Tristan certainly behaves like a man of means."

"Hmm, yes. And what about Bianca?" said the tiny one. "A secretary is generally not worth blackmailing."

Pearl sometimes sounded like some hardboiled old private eye when she talked shop with me like that. Very seriously, very expertly. Or rather *catpertly*, as she would call it.

"What if Laymon wanted something else from Tristan?" Pearl suggested in the next breath. "Not money."

"But what do you have in mind?"

"Maybe his point wasn't the affair between Tristan and Bianca—whether it exists or not—but this strange child that Julia seems to be hiding."

"And this seven- or eight-year-old boy is supposed to have murdered Laymon, then?" I asked skeptically.

"Or what are you actually getting at?"

We were spinning in circles; it felt like I was chasing my own tail.

"Just because he's only seven or eight doesn't mean he couldn't be a killer," Pearl said impassively.

"But he's still so little!" I protested.

"So what? I'm small too, but I'm still a dangerous fighter!"

I did not allow myself to object to this; it would only have ended with another scratch on my nose.

"Think about it," the tiny one continued. "What was that kid doing in Julia's room earlier—besides eating cereal and throwing that bottle off the nightstand? And who's cooking the cereal for him? Julia herself?"

Questions upon questions. My skull ached.

"What if the kid did belong to Laymon?" Pearl went on. She could be really persistent when she was in master-detective mode. "Maybe he saw his father's killer—someone who lives here in this house. That's why the boy snuck into the mansion. To get revenge."

"He's just a little kid, Pearl!" I protested again.

"*Little. Little.* You're just repeating yourself. I would definitely avenge *you* if someone dared to knock you off."

"You would?"

"Sure! I'd scratch his eyes out." She extended her claws demonstratively—which didn't look the least bit frightening. But it was the principle of the thing. I was quite moved.

But then André distracted me with a question he

asked the Chief Inspector: "Do you think poor Edward was involved in something ... that he brought with him here to the island? Something illegal? And that he was killed because of it?"

"That seems like a plausible assumption," Oskar agreed. "We will investigate all leads in that direction, rest assured."

"He actually made a bit of a shady impression," Julia mused aloud to herself, "now that I think about it. But I figured that private eyes can be a bit disreputable and don't always have a spotless record. They are also, uh, sometimes willing to do things that a policeman wouldn't be allowed to do. Only for the good of their clients, of course," she added quickly.

"I can relate," André said. "But to me he didn't even come across as all that shady." He smiled guiltily. "Maybe for old time's sake. I didn't look at him very critically, I'm afraid."

The Chief Inspector nodded thoughtfully, then rose from his chair and took his leave.

"It's getting late," he said. "We'll talk again tomorrow, if that's all right with you. Hopefully we'll know more by then. I've put all my available people on the case and we're investigating at full speed."

Victoria, Pearl and I followed him out of the room.

At the coat rack in the hallway, our two-leggeds put on their jackets. Pearl and I had to slip into our twin harnesses: one large collar, one small collar, and one shared leash that branched out between them. It was inconvenient, because at that moment out of the corner of my eye I noticed movement in one of the hallways—specifically, the one where Julia's bedroom was located. Someone was walking down the corridor, only to disappear right into her room.

Neither Oskar nor Victoria had seen this person, because they were both looking in the opposite direction, towards the front door. Oskar now took a step towards it in order to open it. They were also talking to each other and probably not paying much attention to their surroundings.

I barked and pulled on the leash. The person who had disappeared into Julia's bedroom certainly had no business being there; despite the darkness in the hallway I had been able to recognize who it was: Bianca, the secretary. However, she had quickly closed the door behind her, so that the hallway now lay deserted again.

"Come on, we need to see what she's doing in Julia's room," I explained to Victoria. I pulled on the leash again to emphasize my point.

But Victoria did not understand. "No, Athos stay here," she said sternly. "We really are going home now. Come on."

She pulled relentlessly on the leash, and I had no choice but to comply.

"Strange," I heard Pearl's voice say. Apparently she had seen Bianca as well, but being also already leashed she couldn't go look on her own.

Victoria pushed through the front door, pulling me and Pearl with her out into the night. Once outside in the chill air she stood for a moment, wrapped her scarf more tightly around her neck, and then said goodnight to Oskar.

"I'll get back to you tomorrow," he promised her. "We'll reconstruct Laymon's activities in his last few days, and in the weeks prior to his death, as best we can. He has not to our knowledge rented an office, so he wasn't officially posing as a detective and soliciting clients on a long-term basis. Perhaps he slipped into the role of private investigator only to Mrs. Trapp and her caregiver for some reason."

"And what do you think now? That his death has nothing to do with Julia or her family?" Victoria asked.

"So far, anyway, there's no sign of that," Oskar said. "I rather think he'd messed with one of his own kind—maybe with someone in organized crime who doesn't care that much about human life. The fact that the murderer did him in with a couple of stabs of a knife might indicate that."

"But even if he was a fraud and not a real investigator, he did find out that Tristan was having an affair with his secretary," Victoria pointed out.

"Yes, there is that," the Chief Inspector allowed. "But do you seriously think that's why one of them murdered him? That seems like a bit of a stretch. These are decent people, not members of the mafia."

"But those two aren't having an affair at all!" I barked excitedly. Once again I'd forgotten that communication with our two-leggeds was extremely limited.

Oskar just scratched me behind the ears with a

friendly smile, then finally took his leave of us.

"Let's just make our way home," Pearl said. "I'm starving."

16

The next morning at breakfast Pearl set about devouring a piece of salmon about half her size.

It will never all fit in her stomach, I told myself, but the tiny one nevertheless chowed down as if there were no tomorrow. She behaved as though she had only barely escaped starvation yesterday. Such a little drama queen!

I had eaten a reasonable portion of dog food and was now lying on the sofa next to Victoria, who was chatting on her cell phone with her boyfriend, Tim. He was studying to be an historian in Vienna, so the two of them were currently in a long-distance relationship.

I indulged in a moment of musing on our current case, which may not have been a case at all—at least not for us. It seemed to me that the Harrington family was definitely a powder keg, but maybe in the end these people had had nothing to do with the death of the private detective. Or should I say the pseudo-detective?

Oskar and his colleagues at the police station in Hamburg would probably be able to solve Laymon's murder without us. By now we all suspected that he had been stabbed to death by someone in his petty criminal circle, a scoundrel who had followed him here to the island, persuaded him to go to a nocturnal meeting in the dunes and then killed him there.

Yes, surely that's how the crime had taken place. Here on Sylt, there was not much for us to investigate regarding the motives of the murderer, and Oskar Nüring's colleagues in Hamburg—Laymon's home city—would certainly not request Pearl and me as four-pawed support in solving this case.

Although in theory the idea of snooping around a big city like Hamburg appealed to me, on the other hand I was pretty sure that I liked small places like Sylt better in practice. Unlike Pearl, I loved the great outdoors.

So I assumed that our detective work here was already finished before it had really begun, but still some inconsistencies in the case wouldn't leave my mind. Why had the detective claimed that Tristan and Bianca were having an affair, and even faked evidence to that purpose, when it was not in fact the case? And then this strange child who was hanging around the murder scene and Julia's hotel villa ... that *was* extremely odd and didn't actually fit the theory of a feud among petty criminals.

I dozed off comfortably around noon, and I think I slept for quite a while—until suddenly Victoria's phone shrilled and startled me awake.

Perhaps I was beginning to develop the kind of psychic ability that cats are said to have, but which Pearl clearly lacked. I was suddenly overcome by the feeling that this call did not augur well; even the ringing sounded somehow threatening.

I discarded the thought immediately. After all, I am a sensible dog and do not tend to believe in any hocus pocus—mostly, anyway. As long as we didn't have to deal with ghosts or other spooky creatures.

But I don't want to digress. Anyway, I stretched and yawned, then yelped expectantly at Victoria so that she would quickly accept the conversation.

Pearl was also just waking up from a nap next to me. It was no wonder, after she'd inhaled such a large portion of salmon during her orgy of self-indulgence at breakfast. Her tiny stomach had had to do the digestive work of one like a full-grown elephant's.

"Hello, Oskar," Victoria greeted the caller cheerfully, but the very next moment my gloomy premonition was to prove true.

"What are you saying?" Victoria exclaimed, and she suddenly looked completely shocked. She pressed her cell phone tighter to her ear and at the same time I saw her face had turned chalk white.

I was wide awake in an instant. What on earth had happened? I moved closer to Victoria to try to catch what the Chief Inspector on the other end of the line was saying.

Our two-legged usually turned on speaker phone when listening to calls, but this time she hadn't, much to my chagrin. In fact she even jumped up off the sofa just as I was about to climb onto her lap, and started pacing up and down the room excitedly.

This is why I wasn't able to overhear the conversation at first. Pearl had to run over to Victoria, claw at her pants leg and meow to remind her that we were still there.

Victoria didn't realize that we wanted her to be on speaker, but at least she bent down, took the tiny one in her free hand, and sat down on one of the chairs at the dining table. I trotted over to her and quickly positioned myself next to her ear.

It was fortunate that Oskar also seemed to be very excited. He was speaking so loudly that I could pick up a few of his words. The sharpness of a dog's ear is a fine thing indeed.

"This morning ... an attack," I heard, to my horror. "...my assistant ... already with her at the hospital. I ... unfortunately unavailable ... at home at the moment."

Oh my goodness, that sounded awful.

"*Who* was attacked?" Pearl asked me excitedly. She heard as well as I did, but apparently had also been unable to pick up the name of the perpetrator or his victim.

Oskar must have told Victoria about the victim, but it was probable that the assassin was not yet known. Unfortunately, that's how it usually went regarding acts of violence among the two-leggeds. The humans do not fight honestly and straightforwardly like the lions in the nature documentaries, unceremoniously slamming their paws into their enemies' faces. They usually attack covertly, in secret, in order to avoid the legal consequences.

"Is there anything I can do to help, Oskar?" asked Victoria.

I heard him reply in the negative. Again, I could only pick up a few scraps of words, but enough to understand what the conversation was about. "I hope ... I'm afraid ... maybe talk to Mrs. Trapp together in the evening? Doctors ... no danger to life. But they were concerned ... a drug in her blood that ... did not knowingly take. So ... her nurse André called us. I ... gave him my card yesterday."

"Julia was attacked," I called out to Pearl, and she let out a pitiful meow.

"Poor thing! And we didn't protect her."

Unfortunately it was true. But how could we have managed to spend the night in the actress's villa? Besides, if the perpetrator had given her some drug without anyone being the wiser, how could Pearl or I have prevented it? We probably wouldn't even have noticed him mixing the substance into a drink or her food.

17

Victoria spent the day in restless bustle. She typed out a few emails, chatted with Tim, tried to read a magazine, and asked us several times if maybe we shouldn't visit Julia in the hospital.

"Too pushy, don't you think?" she mused aloud. "Would they even let me see her, since I'm not family? And you two wouldn't be allowed in anyway. Will Oskar have placed a man in the hospital to protect her? Who on earth could have done this to her?"

Pearl and I were asking ourselves the same questions, of course.

Victoria tried to reach Oskar, but he didn't answer the phone. "I'll just have to wait until he calls me," she said to us, looking very unhappy.

It was not until later in the afternoon that the Chief Inspector called again. As far as I could tell Julia had already returned to her villa at the hotel, and Oskar asked Victoria to meet him there.

Pearl and I walked straight to the foyer and placed ourselves by the front door, so that our two-legged would not have the option of leaving without us.

But fortunately she took us along with no objection.

When we met Oskar at the entrance to Julia's villa,

he gave us all quite a scare. He looked as if he himself had only just escaped a poison attack. His hair stood out like straw in all directions, deep dark circles had formed around his eyes, and his skin was paper-white like a vampire's.

Victoria didn't miss it either, of course. She even let out a little scream when she saw Oskar. "For heaven's sake, what happened? Are you sick?" she demanded anxiously.

"Let's talk later," he said in an almost cryptic tone. "We have to take care of Mrs. Trapp first."

Victoria nodded hesitantly. "Is there any news from Hamburg in the meantime, regarding the murder of the detective?" she inquired. "Or rather, the false detective?"

"My colleagues are working on it, but I haven't had any contact with them today as yet." Oskar shrugged apologetically, then ran his hand through his hair, which only made it stick out even further. He covered the last few meters up the garden path to the villa in a few strides and rang the doorbell.

"What's wrong with him?" Pearl asked anxiously. "He didn't even say hello to us."

"He seems terribly scatty. Almost out of his tree," I confirmed. It rarely happened that Oskar failed to lean down and stroke Pearl and me behind the ears a little whenever we met.

Jude Harrington opened the door for us. He also seemed quite startled at the sight of the Chief Inspector, but did not say so aloud.

Only at second glance did I notice that he also made a rather crumpled impression.

"Julia is in her bedroom," he said, "but would it be possible for us to have a short talk afterwards, too, Chief Inspector? I am ... a bit worried. First this murdered detective, and now ... was it really an attempt on Julia's life? And what I actually want to tell you—my wife has disappeared."

"Your wife?" Oskar repeated in alarm. "She's missing?"

Jude hesitated for a moment. "Not precisely," he said finally. "She left—left me. Without giving me the slightest reason, however. I imagine she may have been intimidated, or even threatened? Maybe her life is in danger. And now she won't even return my calls."

I heard Oskar breathing in and out heavily. "Alright Mr. Harrington, I'll talk to you in a minute, okay?" he said. "I just need to speak to Mrs. Trapp first."

"Yeah, sure, no problem." Jude ushered us inside, then disappeared.

"Celeste just took off?" mused Pearl to herself as we followed Oskar and Victoria to Julia's bedroom.

"Do you think she's in danger, too?" I asked.

"Hmm, or maybe she's guilty. Was it perhaps she who wanted Julia out of the way—because of the hotel legacy she's desperate to secure for herself and Jude?"

"Wouldn't it have made more sense to take Tristan out?" I mused.

"Yes, in a way, it would have," the pipsqueak conceded. "But the humans are really not that logical."

Julia was sitting upright in bed, with two thick pillows behind her. She smiled weakly at us when we entered the room. André was hunched on a chair next to her, looking very worried.

"I'm glad you've been allowed to leave the hospital so soon," the Chief Inspector said in greeting.

Pearl dashed between his legs and jumped onto the bed with Julia—where she put on her cuddly kitten act.

Julia's smile widened and she immediately seemed a little less melancholy.

"I discharged myself from the hospital," she told the Oskar. "I hate hospitals. But your assistant visited me, a certain Mr. Kludermann, and I've already told him the most important things."

"Yes, thank you. He filled me in."

"He spoke very little," Julia went on. "Is he always like that?"

"Yes, well, Mr. Kludermann is rather the strong, silent type. *Still waters run deep,* as they say. A thinker, you know." Oskar smiled sheepishly. "I would have come to see you myself, but unfortunately I got held up privately and couldn't make it in time. I'm sorry."

"No problem," Julia said quickly.

Oskar pulled a small notebook from his inside jacket pocket and flipped it open. "Let's go over the events again, please."

He turned to André. "It was you who found Mrs.

Trapp unconscious this morning, Mr. Meissner, here in the bedroom. Correct?"

André nodded agreement. "She'd slept unusually late, didn't show up for breakfast ... so I came to check."

"And you noticed right away that something was wrong? That she wasn't just fast asleep?"

"I'm a nurse, Chief Inspector," André said tersely.

"Quite so, quite so. I didn't mean to criticize you—I just want to get an idea."

"It's all right. I called 911 and Julia was taken straight to the hospital. There it was discovered that her blood pressure had plummeted ... and I insisted on extensive testing to see what might be causing it. Julia had never had problems with her blood pressure before, so it seemed suspicious to me."

Then Julia took the floor: "My father-in-law, Steven—he has high blood pressure, and he takes medication for it. I asked him about it earlier, right after I got back here to the hotel. I was very careful, you know, because I didn't want to offend him at all. He's going to decide in the next couple of weeks which of his sons is going to take over his hotel empire, and I don't want to ruin Tristan's chances by making wild accusations."

"I can well understand that," said Oskar. "And how did he react?"

"Well, I'm afraid he did get a little huffy with me, although I didn't so much as accuse him of the tiniest thing. But when he checked he found that there were actually quite a few pills missing from his antihypertensive."

"Is he sure about that? I'll have to talk to him later," said Oskar.

"Do that. But yes, he's sure."

"He was absolutely distraught about it," André interposed.

Julia nodded in confirmation. "But he himself will hardly have used the stuff on me," she continued. "I certainly don't mean to imply that. It would be too obvious, don't you think? Using your own drugs when you're trying to send someone to the afterlife. Besides, Steven really has no reason to hurt me."

I nervously moved from one paw to the other. A murderer we had all thought too obvious because the deaths pointed too clearly to him—unfortunately that was nothing new to me. Only in our last case had we fallen into exactly this trap, had not even had the killer on our list of suspects, and then we'd ended up with several more murder victims. That must certainly not happen to us again!

"Do you have any idea, Mrs. Trapp, how these tablets were administered to you without you even realizing it?" Oskar went on. "The pills took effect quite quickly, I suppose. Of course, I will still have to check with your doctors at the hospital so we can narrow down the timeline. But did you ingest anything specifically during the night or early morning? Something to drink? Did you eat a snack, perhaps?"

"I wake up fairly often at night," Julia said. "I don't eat

anything in particular, but I like to have a few sips of orange juice. I always have a bottle next to my bed."

"Then you assume that the tablets were dissolved in the juice?" asked Oskar.

"Must have been," Julia agreed. "My doctors claim I wasn't in any real danger of dying, but I think to myself, 'What if I had drunk more than what I did?' If I had emptied the whole bottle, would I be dead right now? Fortunately I only drink a little at a time, and that may have saved my life."

18

"The bottle in question has been disposed of, by the way, Chief Inspector," André added. "So we have no chance to test the contents—and unfortunately, no idea who took it away. When we came back here from the hospital earlier it was gone, even though Julia hadn't drunk it all."

"Has anyone from housekeeping been here to clean up in the meantime, perhaps?" asked Oskar.

I saw him press his lips together, maybe because he blamed himself for not sending an officer here to the villa in time to secure the trace evidence, right after he had learned about the attempt on Julia's life?

What could have kept the Chief Inspector so busy all day that he'd had to leave the case to his more inexperienced assistant? And why did he look so worn out? I licked Oskar's hand anxiously, but he withdrew it from me.

"Yes, housekeeping must have been here," Julia confirmed. "The bed was made when I got back. But I figured that the cleaning ladies wouldn't have thrown away a half-full bottle of orange juice. So I asked André to call housekeeping and check."

"And were you able to find out anything?" Oskar inquired, turning back to the caregiver.

André nodded. "The women who were here today

affirmed that they didn't throw away a bottle—neither an empty one nor a full one. In fact they don't remember there being a bottle on the nightstand at all."

"Then it must have been removed," Oskar said, "before the women cleaned up here. Are you sure the juice was still in place in the morning when you found Mrs. Trapp unconscious?"

"Honestly, Chief Inspector, I didn't pay much attention to it. I thought that Julia..." His words faded away.

That she would die, he had probably wanted to say. One really couldn't blame him for not looking at an orange juice bottle—especially since he couldn't have known at that time that the poison, or rather the potentially lethal drug, must have been in it.

"There's something else you should know, Chief Inspector," André began hesitantly. He glanced at Julia. "Do you want to tell them?"

She frowned. "Well, André, really. It's certainly not relevant, don't you see? Tristan would never—he wouldn't do anything to me!"

André wisely said nothing, while Oskar naturally inquired: "Anything could be important, Mrs. Trapp," he said. "Please let us be the judge. So what actually happened?"

Julia rolled her eyes in annoyance, but then gave him the information. "Oh, last night when I came to bed, I found my orange juice bottle broken on the floor. I don't know how it fell ... but Tristan was with me for a moment then, and he offered to bring me a new bottle. We have a small supply in the fridge in the kitchen so I don't have to keep calling room service."

I saw how Oskar stiffened. Did he smell a clue? I would have liked to explain to him who was responsible for the broken bottle, because Pearl and I had seen the culprit in the act—the strange little boy.

"So your husband brought you a new bottle," Oskar said. "And you drank some juice from it right away, or was it later that night?"

"Not until later in the night—in the early hours of the morning, actually."

"And did you happen to notice if the bottle was still sealed when you opened it? Did the cap crack loose?"

Again Julia grimaced, as if she had bitten into a sour lemon. "The bottle was already open, but that doesn't necessarily mean what you think it means. Tristan didn't tamper with it and dissolve drugs in the juice—he certainly didn't! He's just obliging enough to always open bottles for me. I have quite strong arms and hands, I think, but still I often struggle with these screw caps. I guess I'm just clumsy."

When Oskar did not immediately reply, Julia added emphatically, "Listen, Chief Inspector, my husband certainly didn't put anything in that bottle. I'd stake my life on it."

"How can you be so sure?" asked Oskar.

"How can I be sure?" Julia exclaimed. "Because my husband loves me. He would never hurt me."

"I understand," Oskar murmured.

"Someone else must have tampered with that damn bottle during the night," Julia insisted. "I'm afraid I'm a very deep sleeper; someone could have crept into my room and I certainly wouldn't have noticed. But I can't believe that someone from the family could have—"

She broke off abruptly, and the next moment she hit herself on her forehead with the flat of her hand. "I'm an idiot! It's obvious who's trying to kill me, isn't it? It's Bianca, of course! She ... is having an affair with my husband, you know. Seduced him, that sly little bitch. And she knows I know—I confronted her last night, asked her to quit her job. She must be the guilty one, Chief Inspector! She wanted to get rid of me. Arrest her!"

Victoria managed to look quite astonished at this revelation of Tristan's affair, and Oskar did the same— although of course they had both known about it beforehand. After all, André had already confided in Victoria, and she must have told Oskar. The two of them probably wanted to keep up appearances in front of Julia by acting completely surprised.

"We should have stayed overnight," Pearl insisted. "Then we'd know who poisoned that stupid orange juice." She looked at me seriously, her whiskers twitching.

"And we would once again be racking our brains as to how to communicate it to our two-leggeds," I added.

"Hmm, I suppose so," Pearl grumbled. "That's no consolation, though."

"I'm not saying that. But as for Bianca.... She *was* in Julia's room last night. We saw her."

"Yes. Possibly Julia is right in suspecting her."

"But wait a minute." A thought had popped into my head. "She couldn't have poisoned the bottle that Julia ended up drinking from; Julia said that when she came here to go to bed, her husband found the broken bottle on the floor and brought her a new one. But that must have been later, *after* Bianca sneaked into the room. So how could she have poisoned that juice?"

"Hmm, how about this: when we saw her go into the bedroom, she found the bottle she was trying to poison in shards on the floor and decided to come back later, when there would be a new intact bottle to tamper with?" Pearl suggested.

That was a possibility, of course. Or at least not implausible.

I added, "What if that strange boy wasn't just playing cat when he knocked the bottle off the nightstand? What if *he* was trying to poison her, and he just had a mishap?"

"Excuse me? *Playing cat?*" Pearl's blue eyes narrowed. "What's that supposed to mean?"

"Well, um, you know—you guys do like to throw things on the floor, don't you?"

Pearl said nothing in reply.

"I'm just saying, the kid might have tried to poison the bottle of juice with the antihypertensive," I continued quickly. "Which he'd stolen from Steven. The orange juice slipped out of his hands, and so he returned later that night, and that's when he succeeded in his scheme. When we were long gone, and Julia was fast asleep."

"But the bottle didn't slip out of his hands when we were watching him," Pearl contradicted me. "He threw it down on purpose—like a cat trying to have a little fun," she added, and I suddenly caught an amused look from her.

"That's the impression I got," I said. "But maybe we were wrong. It was pretty dark."

"I see perfectly in the dark," commented the pipsqueak. To which, of course, I had no reply.

Oskar and Victoria said goodbye to Julia for the day, and he promised the actress that he would keep her informed about his further investigations.

"Don't you two want to stay for dinner, maybe?" suggested Julia. "We're eating,"—she glanced at the screen of her cell phone, which was within reach—"in just under two hours. Why don't you be our guests? The cuisine here at the hotel is excellent."

"Thank you, that's very kind of you," Oskar said. "But I ... am needed at home. My wife..." He broke off, nodded sheepishly, and turned to leave without another word.

"His *wife*?" repeated Pearl incredulously.

I was as astonished as she; it was the first time Oskar had mentioned a woman in his life. I had assumed he was single or divorced. After all, he had been making eyes at Victoria for some time, hadn't he? Was he just very friendly with her, and had I misinterpreted that?

I considered myself to be quite an understanding

canine, but at the end of the day, humans are unpredictable. That was definitely not in any doubt.

19

We followed the Chief Inspector out of the room.

Outside in the hallway he said to Victoria, "Let's talk to Jude Harrington about his wife's disappearance. It seems too much of a coincidence that Celeste left him today, of all days—seemingly out of the blue, or so he claims."

Pearl and I trotted after our two-leggeds, and Jude was found momentarily. He had been waiting in the living room for the Chief Inspector and jumped up immediately when we entered the room.

Oskar and Victoria took a seat on the sofa, and after a moment's hesitation Jude sat down as well.

As usual, Pearl and I settled unobtrusively in a corner of the room, where we acted like tired, innocent pets. Jude would never have dreamed that we were registering his every word and secretly discussing whether he was to be trusted, or if he were telling the Chief Inspector a wild tissue of lies.

He made a very serious impression, but that didn't necessarily mean anything. We knew that much from experience.

However, Jude didn't really have much to tell Oskar, except that his wife had left him this morning and hadn't returned his calls since. That was the work of two or three sentences, and didn't necessarily point to another crime we'd have to deal with.

Given the other acts of violence that had already occurred close to this family, Oskar nevertheless promised to contact Celeste Harrington himself to make sure she was safe.

At the end of the conversation, Jude added the following as though it was an afterthought: "By the way, you should also talk to my father-in-law. His girlfriend, Scarlett, wasn't at our joint breakfast today either. Which is most unusual. Until now, she's never been absent from a family meal. Dad didn't elaborate on where she'd gone, and I didn't want to come across as unduly nosy, so I didn't probe further. But why don't you ask him? It can't be right for our ladies to virtually disappear into thin air..."

Oskar promised to look into the matter, but after that he was already preparing to leave the villa.

In the foyer he said to Victoria, "I have to go home I'm afraid, but I'll ask my colleagues to inquire about Celeste and Scarlett. And you and I—we'll catch up with each other later, if it's all right with you?"

"Yeah, no problem," Victoria said.

I could tell that she had a hundred questions on the tip of her tongue about Oskar's wife and the private crisis he seemed to be having. But she did not press him, and he left the villa in a hurry.

"We have to stay here and guard Julia," I said to Pearl firmly. "I'm sure the assassin will still try to complete his murderous work."

"Absolutely," Pearl said, and immediately toddled off

in the direction of Julia's bedroom.

"Haven't you forgotten something, Tiny?" I called after her.

She stopped and turned impatiently to me. "What is it?"

I pointed my head at Victoria, who was by the coat rack, putting on her jacket. "Our human?"

"You can explain to her that we have to stay here, can't you?" Pearl asked calmly, and the next moment she was already prancing off again.

I felt like the butler of an elegant noblewoman. But what can I say, I conveyed to Victoria with eager barking and a few turns around my own axis that Pearl and I could not accompany her home.

And she actually seemed to understand what I was getting at. It was not the first time that Pearl and I had intended to stay behind in the villa.

"You do realize, Athos, that leaving you here is completely insane?" Victoria said to me. "I mean, what exactly are you guys planning? Do I really have to get used to the idea of you two investigating on your own? And that you can do it better than the Chief Inspector?"

She laughed nervously, probably to vent her sense of confusion. "And can you please explain to me why we've seemed to stumble from one murder case right into the next lately?"

I could not.

She sighed, but then seemed to force herself to let Pearl and me do what was necessary, as crazy as it must seem to her.

She leaned down, pressed a kiss on the top of my head and said, "Take care of yourself, will you, big guy? And of Pearl, too. There's a murderer among these people, and maybe he's not an animal lover."

She tickled me behind the ears. "I must be completely crazy to think of leaving you here."

I barked at her again and accompanied her a few steps towards the front door, where I stopped and deliberately sat on my hind paws. What I meant to say quite clearly was: "I'm staying. But don't worry," I added quickly. "Tiny and I will be fine."

I didn't like that our poor two-legged had to worry or even suffer sorrow because of us, but unfortunately that couldn't be changed now. We could not allow Julia to die in this house.

She sighed a second time, but then did what had to be done. "I'll give André a quick heads up that I'm going to have to leave you in his care again," she explained to me. "What excuse am I going to give him this time?"

"You'll think of something," I said confidently.

I looked around for Pearl, who was already scratching at the door of Julia's bedroom to be let in.

It was André who opened the door for her. A smile flitted across his face when he saw us. He bent down, picked up Pearl, then looked down the hall in my direction.

I immediately ran towards him, wagging my tail, and Victoria followed me, quickly sucking the appropriate words out of her thumb.

"I, um, would like to leave my little ones with you and Julia for a brief while longer, if that's okay with you? They're both trained in therapy and will help her recover from the shock."

She didn't mention the fact that we were also experienced bodyguards, but I could live with that.

André was already cradling Pearl's head in his hand, and the little actress was snuggled against his chest, purring.

"How kind of you," he said to Victoria. "These two are really delightful. Julia will be thrilled."

He turned and looked behind him into the bedroom, where Julia was.

He added in a softer voice, "I think she just dozed off, so I'll let her sleep until dinner. Athos and Pearl can help me watch over her." He smiled, but there was definite concern in his expression. He seemed to be entertaining the same thought we were, namely that Julia was far from being out of danger.

"Good idea," Victoria said.

She remained vague about when she would pick us up again, and said goodbye to André.

He carried Pearl into Julia's bedroom, where she hopped from his arms onto the bed and took up position at Julia's feet, her expression that of a royal bodyguard. Strict, fearsome—in her eyes, that is—and determined to do anything to protect her charge.

I made myself comfortable on the bedside rug, where I struck a true Cerberus pose: vigilant, dangerous for anyone who wanted to get too close to Julia. And *truly* terrifying.

I noticed that there was once again a bottle of orange juice on the bedside table. Apparently the actress was determined not to give up her cherished habit, even if she'd almost paid for it with her life.

Julia did not wake up when we joined her.

André took a seat on the chair that stood between the bed and the window, and grabbed the book he'd clearly been reading before. He was a faithful soul and apparently had decided not to let Julia out of his sight from now on. He, like us, did not want to give the vile assassin another opportunity to achieve his goal and end her life.

He read a few pages, but then his eyes sank closed, and Pearl also began to make distinct snoring noises from the bed shortly thereafter.

I myself was also feeling very tired, so I decided to take a spin around the house to get myself going a bit. Julia was in no danger for the moment.

So I sneaked through the door, which I could open by myself, and trotted first through the ground floor and then went upstairs.

I did not meet any of the other family members, and there was also no trace of the child whose parentage was still unknown to us.

Just as I'd returned to the ground floor and turned into the hallway where Julia's room was located, I heard her scream.

The fright put ice into my bones. I sprinted the last

few meters, quickly managed to open the door, and rushed into the room.

Pearl was on her feet, and André had also been roused from his sleep by Julia's call for help. He was bending over her now.

"It's okay, it's all right, it was just a nightmare," I heard him saying. "You're safe."

She struck at him at first, still half asleep, but then she opened her eyes, came to and recognized her nurse-companion.

"I'm sorry," she gasped, "I didn't mean to. Did I hurt you?"

She scrambled up on her elbows, and André pushed a pillow behind her back.

"No, I'm fine," he said. "It was just a silly dream," he repeated soothingly.

Julia brushed her hair out of her eyes with shaky fingers. "I ... don't think it was a dream," she said uncertainly. "I think—I remembered, André."

"Remembered? Remembered what?" he asked.

"Back then...."

"Your accident, you mean to say?"

"Yeah, except it wasn't an accident at all," she whispered.

She stared steadfastly at her caregiver. "I ... remembered, André," she repeated. "I don't know why now, of all times. Maybe those creepy letters are to blame?"

"Excuse me? What letters, Julia?" André reached for her hand. "Are you quite all right? Would you like something to drink?" He took the bottle of orange juice from the nightstand.

The fur on the back of my neck bristled, and Pearl hissed softly.

André suddenly chuckled, even though it was not a happy, lighthearted sound. Rather, it was a groan that gave way to melancholy laughter. We were all quite strung up.

He held the bottle up to Pearl's nose. "Hey there little one, you're an attentive watcher," he said. "That's good. But look, the bottle is still sealed—I checked that earlier. And I took it out of the refrigerator myself."

He turned the lid, and we all clearly heard the crackle that revealed he was speaking the truth.

Julia smiled sadly. "You're really not under any suspicion, André," she said.

Turning to Pearl, she added, "He's one of the good guys, kiddo. He would protect me with his life, so you don't have to worry."

She took a sip from the bottle, and I heard André murmur, "Yes, I would. Any time." He squeezed Julia's free hand briefly but with deep emotion, then let go.

"Should I have a doctor come?" he asked. "Are you feeling unwell? Maybe you left the hospital too soon, after all."

Julia took another sip of orange juice and put the bottle back on the nightstand. "I don't need a doctor, thank you. But I think I'd like to talk to Dr. Adler—I trust her, as she trusts me. Otherwise she would hardly have put her animals in my care, would she? And she's a psychologist, so maybe she can help me make sense of these new memories. Am I imagining everything, after all? Could you call her, André?" Her voice sounded uncertain, almost shaky.

"Yes, of course. Right away," the nurse replied.

20

So it happened that Victoria returned to us earlier than we'd planned. Not twenty minutes had passed before she showed up again at the villa.

We stayed in Julia's bedroom, where our two-legged joined the actress at her bedside.

Julia looked very nervous, even downright anxious, but she began to speak as soon as Victoria had taken her seat.

"Thank you for coming so quickly, Victoria. I really appreciate it. You—I—"

Victoria helped her along. "You had a nightmare? André told me on the phone."

"Yes, I ... that is, no, it was not a dream. I'm sure of that now. I went through a situation that—oh, I don't even know where to begin." She reached for Victoria's hand as if she could hold onto it and thus somehow regain her composure.

"Just tell me what you remember," Victoria said calmly. "Where were you in the dream?"

"At the Black Cliffs Hotel ... a luxury resort off the south coast of England, where we vacationed a few years ago."

"*We*—that is, you and Tristan?" inquired Victoria.

"Not only us. The whole family was present, just as they are here in the hotel together now. Tristan, Jude,

Celeste. Bianca didn't work for my husband back then, and his secretary at the time was not in attendance. Steven was there, but without Scarlett by his side. She wasn't officially his ... partner at the time. His wife was still alive, but she rarely went anywhere with him."

"And what happened in the dream that shook you so badly?" Victoria continued, gently.

Julia's hands were trembling. "There's something you should know about me, Victoria—something that very few people know, and I want to keep it that way. But I can hardly explain the meaning of my dream to you otherwise."

Victoria nodded gravely. "You can rely entirely on my discretion and therapeutic confidentiality, Julia."

The actress sought the gaze of her caregiver, and he nodded. In this way he probably wanted to indicate that he also considered Victoria trustworthy.

Julia cleared her throat, then began: "Um, fortunately, we were able to sweep the matter under the rug as far as possible at the time. Tristan and his father pulled some strings, so that the media only casually mentioned an accident that I suffered on vacation."

"Yes, I read about it too," Victoria said. "Was it at the Black Cliffs Hotel that you had the accident? Didn't you fall off a balcony?"

"Right—except that it wasn't really an accident, Victoria," Julia said.

Our two-legged looked at the actress in amazement, and Pearl's pink nose twitched with tension. The tiny one was so intensely inquisitive, while I....

Oh, who am I kidding, I too was almost bursting with curiosity. What would Julia reveal to us now? *Not an accident*? What, then?

Julia didn't keep us in suspense for long. "The truth is I didn't fall off that balcony," she said. "I jumped."

I heard Victoria draw in her breath sharply.

Julia raised her hands. "Wait, that's not all. I survived the fall into the depths only with very serious injuries. I was in a coma for a few days, and when I regained consciousness, not only did I find that I was a paraplegic, but I also lacked concrete memories. I just knew my name and that I was an actress ... everything else had been wiped out. And my memory has never recovered either, at least until today. I had to listen to my entire past—my whole personal biography—including all the people involved, from the mouths of others and internalize it as if it were just another story. I didn't even recognize my own husband anymore, nor did I know anything about the history of our love and marriage."

"Unbelievable," Victoria said. "And yet you're still married to Tristan."

A tiny smile played around Julia's lips. "I've fallen in love with him all over again, you might say, which to me is a sign that we're actually soulmates."

"A lovely notion," Victoria said, but it didn't escape me that André was frowning rather darkly at Julia's words. And it was not difficult for me to guess his thoughts: soulmates, perhaps only from Julia's point of view, while Tristan was openly cheating on her with other women?

Julia continued: "Until a few days ago, I firmly believed that I had tried to commit suicide at the time, although I didn't remember actually jumping, and of course I didn't recall any motive for this act. Nor had I left a suicide note that could shed any light on the matter. My life before the fall had been perfect, as far as one could tell from the outside. I was celebrating one success after another in my profession, I was married to the man of my dreams ... I never understood why I'd wanted to die at that time."

"And now that's changed?" asked Victoria.

Julia nodded with a thoughtful expression.

"How is that?"

"I've received messages," Julia said. "Here at the hotel. Anonymous letters—yes, I guess that's what you have to call them."

"Julia!" André interjected. "Why didn't you tell me about them? Did they threaten you? That madman who tried to poison you must have written them."

Julia raised her hand defensively. "Not so fast, my dear. I must confess that although the first letter threw me for a loop, I convinced myself that it was not to be taken seriously. I thought someone was playing a macabre joke on me—some crazy fan perhaps."

"That probably explains why she seemed so anxious when we first met her," I said to Pearl. "It wasn't just the detective's death that had gotten to her. She was also scared because she'd gotten an anonymous letter, although she may be downplaying her fear a bit now."

"It's only understandable," Pearl agreed. "Who wants to look like a scaredy-cat?"

"But then, when the second letter came—" Julia continued. However, she immediately broke off again.

After a brief, thoughtful pause, she said, "Well, let's just say I didn't think it was funny anymore. But I don't think those letters were written by the same person who tried to poison me last night—more likely by someone who wanted to warn me."

"Warn you? That you might be attacked?" asked Victoria.

Julia shook her head. "No. I expressed myself poorly. The letter writer probably wasn't trying to warn me directly, but mainly wanted to jog my memory. I think the person who wrote the messages wanted me to remember ... what really happened at the Black Cliffs Hotel."

"So what did the two letters say?" Victoria asked straightforwardly.

21

Pearl indulged in a little more tongue-washing, having brushed her same front paw for about the third time in a row. It was an unmistakable sign of how excited she was. What Julia was telling us sounded like one of those thrillers that the little kitten so loved to watch on TV. I watched the same movies too, of course, but mostly for her sake!

"The first letter contained only three words," Julia said. "*You didn't jump.*"

"'You didn't jump,'" Victoria repeated, as if the words were a magic formula. "Is that all?"

"Yes."

"And how did you interpret that?"

"Well, that I didn't try to commit suicide at the Black Cliffs Hotel."

"And the second letter?" André asked breathlessly.

"That one was even clearer. It said, *You did not try to commit suicide.*"

"Oh my goodness," Victoria said. "So it was an accident after all?"

"I thought so too," Julia said slowly, emphasizing each word, "until earlier today, when I had that nightmare. No, it wasn't quite right—it didn't seem right even before the dream—that I should have suffered an accident, I mean. At the time it was assumed that I had tried to commit suicide. It could not have been an accident, because the balcony railing of our suite at the Black Cliffs Hotel was waist-high. You don't fall over that just because you've slipped..."

"And your nightmare?" Victoria continued quickly. "How did that change anything? What exactly was in your dream?"

Julia cleared her throat again, visibly struggling to get the words past her lips. "I felt two hands in the small of my back."

The curt sentence landed as if Julia had set off a bomb. André let out a strangled cry.

Victoria had only slightly better control of herself. She didn't make a sound, but I couldn't help but notice how her eyes widened radically in shock.

I gave Pearl a little nudge with my muzzle. "Other paw," I murmured to her. "You've been cleaning the left one for half an hour now."

"What?" The tiny one stared at me. Her blue eyes were also even bigger than usual.

Then she took on the grooming of her right paw, but at the same time, at least outwardly, she found herself back in her role as master detective.

"If Julia felt two hands against her back, that means she was pushed," she explained to me, although of course I had long since figured that out for myself—and all without the excessive care routine.

"An attempted murder, then," she said, "and not a suicide. And now her life is in danger again. The same culprit must be behind it, don't you think, Athos?"

"He sure took his sweet time," I pointed out.

"He may not have had a chance ... until now." Pearl licked devotedly over both her paws, which were now oozing cleanliness. But that wasn't actually the point of this grooming session at all.

"None of what I just told you must leak out, Victoria," Julia implored our two-legged. She sounded like she was halfway over the shock of the nightmare now and more in control of herself. Although right after that she clasped her hands in her lap and kneaded them as if she were trying to create a loaf of bread.

"Don't worry, no one will hear a single word from my lips," Victoria said, and while I wondered if that included the Chief Inspector, Julia seemed content to let it go.

Our human is very good at exuding trustworthiness. And she makes people feel that they can really solve their problems just by getting them off their chest. It is her super power—which is just like the ones often featured in movies.

Supposedly every human being has such a power, not just those guys who call themselves Superman, Spider-man, Iron Man or something like that. And we animals do too, of course, although people often forget that or don't even realize it.

What is my super power, you may ask?

The answer is: I am an excellent protector. Even though I have my paws full and often reach my limits with both Victoria *and* Pearl. The two of them have an amazing talent for getting themselves into difficult, if not life-threatening, situations. And they do it all the time.

And Pearl's super power? Eating salmon?

No, I don't want to do the tiny one an injustice. She can truly do much more than that.

Pearl is capable of taking almost any human heart by storm, no matter how hardened it may be. And she is a very good comforter. I can also say the same about myself. With me, however, my comfort sometimes gets a little moist, because I distribute hand- or even better ear-kisses for this purpose—which unfortunately not everyone appreciates.

Oh, and she's brave too, of course, my miniature tigress. Even if her courage may sometimes border on a recklessness that's weary of living.

"How did you actually come to receive the two letters, Julia?" Victoria continued now. "They didn't just come in the mail or via email, I assume?"

"No, they were delivered to me personally here, at the hotel. The envelope in each case was labeled only with my name, and it was slipped under the front door unseen. I discovered the first letter myself in the hallway shortly after we arrived here, and the second was brought to me by Bianca, but she too claimed to have found it under the door. That was only last night. And I think to myself—well, couldn't it be that these two letters have jogged my memory? Could they be the reason I had that horrible dream today, where I was pushed off the balcony? That would be quite possible from a psychological point of view, wouldn't it ... or even probable?"

Victoria did not answer right away. She seemed to be weighing her words carefully.

"Quite possibly," she said finally. "Perhaps your memory really has returned, but it may also be a false remembrance—an implanted memory—brought about through these letters, you understand. You must not take your dream unquestioningly at face value."

"Yeah, maybe," Julia muttered.

Victoria eyed her attentively, but when Julia didn't continue, she asked a new question. Or rather, she mused aloud: "If the letters were slipped under the door, then unfortunately any outsider could be the letter writer, someone who lives or even works here in the hotel, and who recognized you—which should not be difficult. Your face is well known all over Germany."

"And beyond," André said. He was really very proud of his employer, there was no mistaking that. Taking care of her was more than just a job for him.

Pearl seemed to have come to the same conclusion regarding André's devotion and, as she so often did, had a practical solution to hand. Or rather to her carefully-licked paw, I should say. "If Julia's husband does cheat on her, or at any rate doesn't love her as much as she loves him, then she should go for this nurse," the pipsqueak opined. "André is so nice, he looks good, smells good..."

"But he doesn't have any salmon in the fridge, just regular sausage," I pointed out.

Pearl's blue eyes narrowed. "Are you making fun of me, Athos?"

"What are you thinking? I would never allow myself to do that! On this dog's honor!"

I gave her a gentle nudge with my nose, then we listened again to the humans' conversation, which was still not finished.

"What if Celeste wrote me those letters?" Julia said to Victoria. "She was there at the Black Cliffs Hotel back then. Maybe she heard or saw something...?"

"And kept quiet about it until today? For several years?" said Victoria.

"Yes, it is strange, you're right. But she disappeared today—or at least left precipitously. That's what Jude claims, anyway. I saw him briefly earlier when I came back from the hospital. They say Scarlett's gone too. Doesn't that strike you as suspicious?"

"Yes, I must say it does," Victoria admitted.

Julia nodded, but the next moment she twisted the corners of her mouth downwards. "Scarlett, however, was not with us when we were vacationing at Black Cliffs. But even she might have—I don't know, picked up something—from Steven, maybe? Perhaps she drew the right conclusions from something that he overlooked? Although my father-in-law really is not a stupid man."

22

"I have a suggestion for you, Julia," Victoria said. "A procedure that might jog your memory, now that it seems ready to allow certain traumatic events of the past to resurface, if that's what you really want. And—with your permission—I would like to tell Chief Inspector Nüring about these letters you've received. We can't keep a clue like that from him if he's to find out who tried to kill you last night. I promise you he will treat all information with one hundred percent discretion."

"If you trust him..."

"I do, Julia."

"Okay—and as for my memory, of course I want to remember! Apparently someone really was trying to kill me back then, damn it!"

"That's what it looks like, unfortunately," Victoria confirmed.

"What do I have to do?" asked Julia. "What do you propose?"

"I would like to suggest one or more sessions of hypnotherapy. I find it to be one of the most effective methods when it comes to bringing buried memories to light. I want to try to take you back in trance to that balcony, to find out what really happened there. Up front I have to say there's no guarantee that it will work, or how much you'll be able to recover from your lost memories—and the experience could be, well, upsetting."

"I don't care," Julia replied. "I'm already agitated anyway. But hypnosis—that's what they tried on me at the hospital back then, when I was undergoing treatment after the fall—or suicide, as they assumed it to be at the time. It didn't really do anything to help."

"I can't give you any guarantee that it will work now either," Victoria said, "but the fact that certain memories seem to be coming back on their own is a good sign. I think now is the right time to try hypnosis again. And I must say that I've had some success using it with my patients."

"Alright, I'm in," Julia said. "What have we got to lose, right? I want to know who's trying to kill me, and I'll do anything to jog my memory!"

"Well, we could do the first session tomorrow if you'd like," Victoria allowed.

"Yes, that sounds good. But as for tonight, you really must stay for dinner now that you're here. I'd really appreciate it."

"Then I gladly accept your invitation," Victoria said.

"She wants to snoop, our assistant detective," Pearl noted with satisfaction. "And we will too, of course."

"Besides, I'm sure she'll get you a proper dinner this time," I added. I had to make the remark; I just couldn't help myself.

I earned a critical look from her narrowed blue eyes, and returned the gesture with a wet tongue-kiss on the adorable snub nose of my pipsqueak. Whereupon *my* poor nose once again caught a few scratches. Eh well, it's clear I'm really not capable of learning.

I was to be proven right about the culinary component of the evening—when it came to placing orders with room service at the joint dinner, which was to take place again here in Julia's villa, she was kind enough to ask Victoria about our taste preferences as well.

So Pearl got her fried fish, and I got a big piece of roast lamb. And ice cream for dessert! Dog heaven! I am by no means such a picky eater as the tiny one is, but then I wouldn't spurn a good meal either.

Also at the dinner were Jude, Steven, Tristan and Bianca. Celeste and Scarlett's seats at the large dining table remained empty, and no one commented on the whereabouts of the two women.

There was much eating and drinking, but very little conversation.

Julia's stare at Bianca was downright hostile, while the latter and Tristan avoided the actress's angry glance as best they could.

Outside the windows, where it had long been pitch dark, it had begun to snow. Flakes danced through the darkness and were swirled around wildly by an oncoming storm. It was the kind of night you wouldn't chase a dog out into—or so the humans chose to phrase it. I, on the other hand, wouldn't have minded a romp across a fresh blanket of snow in this cold and stormy weather.

Pearl on the other hand devoured her entire portion of fish and then curled up on a fauteuil near the dining table for a nap. I too would have liked to close my eyes for a bit, after having gleefully savored my ice cream, but someone had to stay alert in this house. I watched the people at the table and wondered the whole time which of them could be out to end Julia's life.

The most obvious answer was probably Bianca—at least she had a motive to do away with Julia, if she really were out to steal her husband and his future hotel inheritance. But tonight, in Julia's actual presence, she seemed more intimidated than murderous. And besides, she hadn't been there on the fateful vacation at the Black Cliffs Hotel, where Julia had been attacked once before.

Yet another tricky case! Although there are probably no simple murder cases, or at least Pearl and I had never encountered one before.

As the waiters from room service came back, clearing the plates and serving coffee and spirits in their place, Julia turned to Victoria.

"I think you should stay over tonight," she suggested. At that, she gestured toward the window. And what did she say next? Of course: "You couldn't chase a dog out the door in this weather. And we do have a spare bedroom here in the house."

Victoria hesitated slightly before finally accepting with thanks. I had the suspicion that she really did want to stay here—presumably to be near Julia and thus prevent another attack on her life.

"I'm also happy to have Athos and Pearl staying with me," Julia added. "These two are a real comfort to me. Such lovely animals."

23

Around ten o'clock in the evening, Oskar called Victoria's phone and promised to stop by before she went to sleep in the guest room.

When he arrived, Victoria received him in the smaller living room upstairs. Did she have any qualms about inviting him into her bedroom? I was not sure.

But tonight there was not the slightest hint of the romantic tension that usually sizzled between the two of them. When Oskar appeared, he still looked like a beaten dog—hmm, again a doggy metaphor. How did I always manage to come up with them?

His shirt was wrinkled, his lips dry and chapped, and he dropped down on the sofa next to Victoria with a deep sigh.

"What a day," he groaned.

"Do you want to tell me all about it?" Victoria asked gently. "About your ... wife? You never mentioned you were married before." Sometimes she really knew how to get bluntly to the point.

Oskar let himself sink further into the upholstery of the sofa and closed his eyes. "I really didn't mean to hide anything from you, Victoria. It's just—she's very ill, and the only way I can bear her suffering now is by being in denial as much as possible. At least when I'm on duty. It's probably terribly selfish of me, but it doesn't help her if I beat myself up over her illness, you see. I have to be there for her, and I can only do that if I don't let myself sink into depression. And at work ... I have to clear my head somehow, otherwise I might as well hand in my notice."

Victoria took his hand. "I'm so sorry," she said. She didn't probe any further, didn't ask any of the countless questions that must have been on the tip of her tongue, as much as they were on mine.

I put my muzzle on Oskar's knee, and Pearl hopped onto the sofa between the two humans.

She meowed at the Chief Inspector: "You can tell Victoria everything. She's a good comforter—almost as good as me."

In the next moment she was snuggled up against Oskar's arm and purring devotedly, putting a little smile on his face as if to prove her words.

"Denying everything doesn't really work, of course," Oskar said. "Or at least only partially. And I can't tell myself that it might get better someday, either. My wife is only forty-two years old, but she already suffers from dementia; an early form that progresses rapidly and is incurable."

"Oh Oskar," Victoria said. "How awful. I'm so sorry."

He nodded, barely noticeably. "On her best days, Marianne still recognizes me, but on her worst days..." He shook his head. "That's when she's tormented by a terrible paranoia, and thinks everyone wants to hurt her. And then she fights us with vigor, unfortunately. We have a great care team that lives with us—two women who take turns, so Marianne doesn't have to live in a home, and I can be with her. But sometimes it's all quite beyond my strength, I'm afraid."

"Today was one of Marianne's bad days?" said Victoria, but the question was probably more rhetorical. A blind man could have read the answer from the look on Oskar's face.

"Very bad," he said. "It's never been like this before. She got extremely aggressive, attacking her nurse, hitting the poor woman with her fists ... and then me, too, when I tried to calm her down."

He took a deep breath. "Let's talk about something more pleasant, shall we? Our murder case." The corners of his mouth tightened. "It sounds crazy, but it really does feel that way."

At that moment there was a knock at the door, and when Victoria called out "Yes?" Bianca entered the small living room.

She carried a silver tray on which stood several steaming cups that were giving off the delicious aroma of chocolate.

My mouth watered. I got to my feet, but Bianca just laughed and lifted the tray out of my reach.

"Hot chocolate," she announced. "I think we can all use some today. Would you like a cup?" She turned to Oskar and Victoria.

Both of them reached for the tray. Pearl made no attempt to grab a cup, and I went empty-pawed as well. "I heard that chocolate is dangerous for dogs," Bianca said to Victoria. "Is that true?"

"Yes, unfortunately," our two-legged replied. "Cocoa can be toxic to dogs even in small amounts. Although Athos certainly wouldn't be averse to a cup, would you, my good fellow?"

She reached out her hand to me and tickled me behind the ears. I enjoyed that quite a bit, but the fact that I wasn't allowed to have chocolate was just unfair, I thought. If the stuff is that harmful to dogs, why does it smell so darn tempting? Not fair indeed!

Oskar and Victoria sipped their hot drinks and sat there still and silent, even after Bianca had long since left the room.

"Is there anything I can do for you, Oskar?" said Victoria finally. "Or for your wife? I would love to help you any way I can. I can't say I have much experience with dementia patients, but I could read up on the kind of psychological care that might help."

Oskar raised his head and looked her directly in the eye. "You already do so much for me, Victoria, don't you realize that? And I don't mean that you support me at work. You do that too—a lot. You and your little zoo." He gently tapped his index fingertip on Pearl's nose as she looked up at him.

"Your work is so very exciting to me," Victoria said. "I'm glad you let me share in it, and I..." Her voice suddenly failed. "You are a wonderful person, Oskar. I had no idea you were married, and you know I have a boyfriend whom I love very much. Because if I didn't, I would ... oh, I don't know." She broke off abruptly again.

Oskar put down his cup and took her hand. "Tim must be a really great guy; you've told me so much about him. And my wife and I, we were like peas in a pod once, too. A dream team. Once upon a time.... Now she's gone, albeit not physically, but it's not the same. I miss her; it feels like I've already lost her, though not to death. On the one hand, I'm grateful she's still with me—at least partially—but on the other hand her fate is in many ways worse than death. I myself wouldn't want to live like this, but I can't even ask her anymore what she would choose if she were still mentally capable of making that choice."

He swallowed. "I'm lonely, Victoria. And you're ... oh, damn. I should go."

He let go of her hand as if it had burned him and stood up with a jerk. "I'll see you tomorrow, okay? Take care of yourself tonight, please."

He looked down at me. "You keep an eye on her, promise me that, buddy. And on Tiny, too." He gave Pearl a sweet smile, even if it came across as rather melancholy.

"Did he just call me *Tiny*?" protested Pearl.

"I know, only I am allowed to say that," I replied.

"No! No one is allowed to say it. I'm not tiny—just not very tall."

"It's all right, Ms. Tiger Queen," I said quickly, and that soothed my prickly little friend.

Oskar held out his open hand to me in farewell, and I solemnly put my paw in it. "You can count on me," I said. "And give your poor wife an extra wet ear-kiss from me."

"Wait, Oskar," Victoria said abruptly, "there's something I want to talk to you about before you go. I almost forgot—because of what you've just told me. But it's important!"

She pulled the Chief Inspector back onto the sofa, and then a somewhat chaotic report bubbled out of her. She told Oskar all that Julia had confided to her, albeit in rather confused sentences. She smelled very agitated, that much was impossible to ignore.

She talked first about the anonymous letters Julia had received, then about her alleged suicide attempt at the Black Cliffs Hotel, which had turned out to possibly not have been one at all, and finally about the dream in which she had even physically felt someone pushing her off the balcony at that time—even though Julia couldn't say who that person had been. The same killer who was now taking a second chance to send the actress into the afterlife?

When Victoria had finished her report, Oskar pressed his lips together firmly.

"This is bad," he said. "We have to therefore assume that Mrs. Trapp was supposed to have been murdered at that instant. Hopefully, through your planned hypnosis sessions, you will be able to clarify whether there is any truth to these memories that have so suddenly beset her—and to the claims made by this anonymous letter writer. If she truly was attacked back then, I would also assume it's the same person who is trying to kill her now. Unless she's guarding some secret that she won't reveal to us, but which is causing several different people to want her dead.... No, that's probably too far-fetched."

"On the other hand, she can't remember her past at all. Her entire life before the fall," Victoria said. "But I also don't rate her as someone who has any skeletons in her closet. I can't see a single psychopathic trait in her."

Oskar straightened up and tightened his shoulders. "Victoria, we ought to put her under police protection. She's not safe in this house—and neither are you. If you try to take care of Julia while standing in the way of the killer, he may not hesitate to eliminate you also. And I could never forgive myself if anything were to happen to you. Losing you too..." He moaned softly and pressed his lips together so tightly that his jaw muscles bulged.

"You don't have to worry," Victoria said. "André told me that he will sleep in the armchair in Julia's room tonight, and Athos will sound the alarm if anyone sneaks through the house in the darkness. Nothing will happen to us, Oskar."

"I still don't like it," he grumbled. But his resistance was very weak. He had to be dead tired after this long and difficult day. The rings around his eyes had turned a deep, dark color by now, and he got to his feet only with difficulty as he went to take his leave.

He kissed Victoria tenderly on the cheek in farewell. "Thank you for everything. I'm so glad you exist," he said.

Victoria smiled uncertainly. And now it was he who thought of something else. "Oh, I wanted to tell you one more thing—my colleagues were able to locate Scarlett Bishop. She's fine. She left the hotel voluntarily, by her own admission, supposedly because of the new inheritance arrangements announced by Steven Harrington. We are still checking when exactly she left Sylt, but according to her information it was very early yesterday morning. She would still have had the opportunity the night before to mix Steven's blood pressure medication into Julia's orange juice, but a motive for such an act is not yet apparent to us. Good night, Victoria."

We accompanied him to the door, where Victoria wrapped herself in jacket and scarf and left with me for a short walk.

Pearl bravely joined us, even though the full-blown snowstorm that was by now sweeping across the island almost knocked her off her paws.

I tried to play around with her a bit. The snow that covered the front yard of the house was so fluffy, and wonderfully cold.

She joined in half-heartedly at first, but then seemed to start enjoying stretching her paws and having a little fun instead of just thinking about murder and mayhem. And of Oskar's poor wife.

Victoria watched our play and walked a few steps through the snow herself. However, she seemed very tired and soon called us back to her to finish our walk.

24

When we returned to the house, an ugly surprise awaited us. Under the door of Victoria's guest bedroom there was a letter. The envelope looked inconspicuous and it had no stamp.

Victoria picked it up, opened it and skimmed through the contents. The next moment a strangled cry escaped her, and she dropped the sheet as if it had burned her fingers.

Neither Pearl nor I could read the words, but there had to be something hideous in this letter, something that frightened Victoria, but which at the same time had infuriated her.

She pushed us into the room, closed the door and dug out her cell phone. Her movements were slow and erratic. She must be dead tired, even if the letter had startled her out of her skin.

"I'll call Oskar," she explained to us. She liked to talk to us when she was alone, a kind of soliloquy before an audience that she still didn't entirely trust to understand her words.

The call rang for a long time until Oskar finally answered. I ran up close to Victoria and Pearl jumped onto her lap to hear what he was going to say. This time Victoria actually understood our intent and put him on speaker phone.

"Are you all right?" asked Oskar. "I just got home—I almost fell asleep in the car." He yawned.

"I've been longing for bed, too," Victoria said, "but I'm pretty darn awake now."

She told him about the letter, then read it to him.

Better you don't interfere, you disgusting snoop. The neck of a little kitten breaks so easily.

"What?" his voice boomed from the phone at full volume. Apparently, the Chief Inspector was now wide awake too. "How dare he, that stupid pig! I'll wring *his* neck!"

"I guess someone really doesn't want me to help Julia remember," Victoria said. Her voice quivered. "It's all right, Athos, calm down," she reprimanded me gently. "No one is going to get hurt. We'll get that bastard!"

I had not noticed how angrily I had growled, but now I pulled myself together. In my shock I licked Pearl so wetly over her snout that she in turn protested loudly.

"Hey, you can't slap your tongue in my face like that!" She shook herself vigorously as if she had just climbed out of the bathtub.

Well, maybe she had gotten a *little* wet.

"Sorry," I grumbled. "But nobody's going to break your tiny neck! Over my dead body!"

For once I didn't have to listen to Pearl say that she didn't need a canine bodyguard. Instead, she actually nestled her head against my chest.

"Wow," Victoria said to Oskar, staring at us in puzzlement. "It seems to me that my pets have realized what the letter is about. They're all over the place."

"Who had the opportunity to plant the letter?" asked Oskar. He sounded more composed now, but his voice still vibrated with anger.

"It must have happened in the last hour or so," Victoria said. "I was in here earlier, and I'm sure the letter wasn't by the door then. It would have been impossible to miss it. Afterwards you and I talked in the living room, and then I was just outside for a minute with Athos and Pearl."

"It's unlikely that anyone would have entered the house from the outside during that time," the Chief Inspector said. In the same breath he added, "Listen to me, Victoria—I want you to leave this villa, along with Ms. Trapp. Right now. Move to another hotel, and take Mr. Meissner with you—he looks pretty capable of self-defense to me when it comes down to it. Don't tell anyone else in the family where you're going. I don't care what excuse Mrs. Trapp has to make up for doing it; I'm sure you'll think of something. Call me as soon as you've moved, and I'll put two uniforms in front of the hotel you've chosen. Just in case. I would come over myself, but I dare not leave Marianne alone with her nurse tonight. Otherwise I might have an assault victim on my hands here, too. Besides, I could fall asleep standing up—I don't know what's wrong with me. But I'll call two constables right now and send them over to you."

"What good are two men positioned in front of the house when the murderer is possibly living here with us under the same roof?" Victoria mused.

"I was going to say that I'll send the officers to your new hotel. You'll have to get Mrs. Trapp to move."

"It's a quarter to twelve, Oskar. She may already be asleep."

"Then wake her up, please, Victoria. You can't take this situation lightly. I'd never forgive myself if that bastard made good on his threat and something happened to you—or to your kitten."

"Nice man," Pearl opined. "I've been saying for the longest time that he should be part of our family."

"He's married," I objected. "We know that now."

"Yes, but his wife.... Never mind, let's catch this killer. We should stay here and draw him out. This is our chance! We don't have anything else to use against him, so let him come; I'm not afraid of him."

"He *or she*," I said. "If we have to look for the murderer among the residents of this house, then only Bianca and Tristan have real motive."

"I'm going to check on Julia," Victoria told Oskar, "and try to get her to move."

"Fine, please call me back later."

"You should go to sleep," Victoria said, unable to suppress a yawn herself.

"Call me," Oskar insisted. "I don't care what time it is."

"Please don't worry if she doesn't want to move. I have Athos with me—he will take care of us. All of us."

"Julia was poisoned with a drug," protested Oskar. "Your dog can't protect you from such an attack."

Victoria suddenly fell silent.

"What is it?" Oskar asked in alarm.

"I'm just thinking about all the things I ate and drank here at the villa tonight. At dinner ... and then Bianca brought us the hot chocolate. You had some, too. And I must confess that I didn't think for a moment that something could possibly be administered to us that way. But we're fine," she quickly added. "Everything's alright, I think. No symptoms of poisoning."

"Oh God, Victoria, it could be a slow-acting poison," Oskar replied. "I wasn't paying attention either, I admit. I was so—I can't think straight."

"No, no, don't blame yourself. It's all right now. I feel fine; just very tired. I don't know if I could handle moving to another hotel tonight."

"You have to try! Please go and talk to Mrs. Trapp. Right now."

Victoria yawned again. Neither she nor Oskar seemed to be themselves anymore—just two dead-tired robots who were completely beside themselves and could no longer think or even act properly. Everything had become too much for them, that much was clear. And I didn't like it at all.

Pearl let herself be infected by Victoria's yawns. She opened her tiny jaws wide, which amused me greatly. But right after that she was already pattering toward the door. "I'm off to see Julia," she said.

I joined her, and Victoria ended the call and followed us.

It was not far to Julia's bedroom. Our two-legged knocked on the door, at first timidly, then quite energetically. When nobody opened even after the third attempt, she turned the door handle. The interior doors here in the villa had no locks, so they could be opened without hindrance. In a dream vacation hotel on a remote, romantic island, no one assumes that guests would have to fear for their lives.

Cautiously, Victoria pushed open the door. A little light fell into the room from the hallway behind us, and a small lamp was burning on one of the nightstands, illuminating with difficulty only one corner of the room. There André sat—or rather slouched—on his chair. He was fast asleep. At his feet I spied an open book that had probably dropped out of his hands. Julia was lying in the bed and had also fallen asleep.

Victoria hesitated. She yawned again, but then forced herself forward and prepared to wake the two sleepers. She touched André on the shoulder until he startled up with a grunt and at first didn't seem to know where he was at all.

"I'm so sorry, but I need to talk to Julia," Victoria explained to him. "At the Chief Inspector's request."

"What, why ... what happened?" stammered André.

"I'll wake her up, okay?" said Victoria.

He didn't try to stop her, but instead got to his feet, trying to rub the sleep out of his eyes.

It took a long time for Julia to finally open her eyelids. She pulled herself up on her elbows, leaned against the head of the bed and stared at Victoria in confusion.

Our poor human was yawning again, but then she managed to convey the contents of her phone call to the Chief Inspector, as well as his urgent request that the actress find another hotel tonight.

"Move? Now? Are you crazy, Victoria?"

André sat down on the opposite edge of the bed. "I think it's a sensible idea, Julia. We can't be too careful."

"I wanted to talk to the Chief Inspector anyway, first thing in the morning," the actress said, evading the topic. "Earlier when I went to bed I noticed that some valuable pieces were missing from my jewelry box. A diamond necklace and a matching brooch. Also, two rings, one of them a five-carat."

"Excuse me?" Victoria said. She really hadn't expected that, and neither had I. A jewelry theft? In the middle of a murder case?

"Could it be that you just, um, misplaced the pieces?" asked Victoria.

"I'm paralyzed, not senile, my dear," Julia returned acerbically. "But as I said, it can wait until tomorrow morning."

"We really should heed the Chief Inspector's advice and move to another hotel," Victoria said, making another fairly desperate attempt. She blinked as she spoke, as if she could barely keep her eyes open.

Julia's jawline hardened. "How do you imagine that? And how am I supposed to explain it to my husband—

or to his father, who is currently keeping a close eye on him while he decides to whom he should leave his entire fortune? Tristan and I have to demonstrate we're a good team so that he will inherit the hotel chain. What impression would Steven receive if I fled his hotel in the middle of the night? And do you want to read in tomorrow's paper that I'm afraid of my own family?"

"I understand your concern," Victoria countered, "but surely your life is worth more to you than your image?"

"My life? Then why doesn't your dearest Inspector finally arrest that little tramp? Huh? She's behind it, I tell you—Bianca! She's out to kill me. And she'll undoubtedly try again if he doesn't finally put a stop to her!"

"She wasn't there at the Black Cliffs Hotel, though," Victoria said in a curt tone. She is the sweetest of two-leggeds, but now she seemed to be running out of patience.

Julia stared angrily at Victoria. She probably didn't like the conclusion that was hovering in the air one little bit. If Bianca was not the culprit, there was only one other suspect left who was in the house right now.

Julia had to be aware of that fact, as well. Finally she hissed and said, "No! Tristan would never hurt me, if that's what you're getting at. We have our ups and downs as in any long marriage. But he loves me!"

Victoria sat perplexed for a moment, then sighed. "Okay, then we'll just have to stay here. André is with you, after all ... and if the slightest thing should happen, the slightest noise, call me immediately, will you?"

She pushed Julia's cell phone, which was on the nightstand, closer to the bed. Then she pointed to the full bottle of orange juice sitting next to it. "Still sealed, I hope?"

"Yes, of course. I'm not stupid." Julia rubbed her eyes and tried to smile. "Look, I'm sorry. I know you mean well, but really I'm quite safe. Go to sleep, my dear. I'll talk to you in the morning."

André pulled up the blanket so Julia's shoulders were covered, then returned to his chair.

"Good night, Victoria," he echoed, and with that we began our retreat to our bedroom.

Victoria called the Chief Inspector again, as promised. It rang for a long time, but he did not pick up. Our two-legged hung up.

"We should let him sleep," she said. "What do you think? I'm sure we'll be really safe for tonight."

I sat up on my hind legs, assuming my watchdog pose, and assured her that she could count on me.

She smiled tiredly. "But honestly, my little ones, I really don't understand what's going on anymore—first that dead detective, who wasn't one at all, then the attempt on Julia's life. And now a jewel robbery? Plus anonymous letters, two women who just up and leave, and this threatening letter to me. And Julia's memories, which seem to be slowly coming back. Does any of it make sense anymore?"

25

The world outside the villa was slowly but surely turning into a polar landscape. The wind howled around the house, making the thatched roof creak and groan, and the snowflakes were falling so thickly by now that you had the impression of staring into a swirling white sea when you looked through the window.

At some point despite my best intentions I was overcome by sleep, but I think it was short-lived. Victoria's snoring woke me up, and I got back up onto my paws. My body felt heavy as lead.

I decided to take a turn around the place. Waking Pearl for this was unnecessary; she was curled up next to the door, like a miniature tiger trying to be a guard. I walked over to her, opened my muzzle, and gently scooped her up like a little puppy. Then I carried her to the bed and put her in the crook of Victoria's arm.

"I'll be right back," I said. "Take care of each other."

"Mmm-hmm..." she mumbled without really waking up.

I walked through the villa's dark corridors, where all was quiet except for the howling snowstorm outside that rattled the roof and shutters.

I stopped by Julia's bedroom, where I pressed down the handle and silently poked my head through the doorway. André was asleep in the armchair, and the actress was lying in bed, breathing quietly.

So far so good—I walked on. This villa really was very spacious.

To my astonishment, as I passed by Tristan's study upstairs I noticed a streak of light under the door. I also heard soft voices coming from the room. Tristan and a woman ... Bianca, I assumed.

Here, too, I managed to operate the door handle and gain access to the room. But I was not made welcome.

"Hey, what are you doing here?" Bianca greeted me, in a less than friendly tone. So she was indeed the one whose voice I had heard; I had not been mistaken.

The secretary and her boss seemed to be working at a very late hour. Both were sitting at the desk, in front of open laptops.

Tristan rose, came up to me, and waved his arms in front of my muzzle. "Shoo, shoo, out you go!"

I dropped stubbornly to the floor and made myself out to be a very tired dog. He tried to push me, but I was quite immobile. Sometimes it is an advantage that I have such a thick coat and look much heavier than I really am.

"Has your wife adopted this dog now? And the cat that goes with it?" Bianca asked in an amused tone.

"I don't know. Looks like it," said Tristan.

"Well, I've never seen such a massive husky before, anyway," she quipped.

I had a good mind to bare my teeth and scare her a little, but I didn't let on—otherwise they would have ended up trying even harder to get me out of the room. I, however, wanted to observe what they were doing here so late at night. What were they talking about?

Were they planning something evil? Another attack on Julia? Or even on Victoria, because she had interfered and wanted to help the actress to remember again? If so, they should be prepared to deal with this massive husky ... who in reality was a slender and very good-natured Malamute, but who took a very dim view when his two-legged and his tiny one were threatened.

The two worked on their computers for a few more minutes, but didn't seem to actually be plotting anything. I was almost disappointed. One of them had to be the murderer we were looking for, surely?

Apparently they were not in cahoots after all. They mentioned absolutely nothing that could have been interpreted as a threat.

To all appearances they were still working on the blog article about the hotel we were staying at, which they were going to post on Tristan's website. When they finally finished, Bianca closed her laptop and Tristan stood up.

"Whew, that took forever," he said. "I could really use a drink right now."

"There's still whiskey in the dining room, I think," Bianca said. "Shall I get you a glass?"

"That's very sweet of you, but I'm really not in the mood for whiskey right now. More like something sparkling. But I guess there's no room service so late."

He glanced at his wristwatch. "Well, never mind."

He sat down again and his gaze wandered over Bianca's legs. I lifted my head to see better, but fortunately did not draw any attention to myself. The two humans only had eyes for each other.

"By the way," Tristan began after a minute of somewhat embarrassed silence, "I haven't told you yet—Jude came to see me today. He proposed a deal with me, wanted us to split the company down the middle, no matter who Father ends up bequeathing it to now."

Bianca looked pleased. "An unmistakable sign that you have the advantage—and that your brother is well aware of it."

Tristan smiled and his fingers stroked Bianca's arm, as if of their own volition. She didn't pull away, just stiffened a little.

"Well," he said, "Father doesn't appreciate Celeste leaving at all. He values wives who support their husbands—who stand behind them the good old-fashioned way."

"Yet apparently Scarlett has taken off, too," Bianca said. "He must be pretty embarrassed."

"Oh certainly," Tristan said. "I think Scarlett left because he sort of disinherited her; she always was after his money, or so it was perfectly clear to me. And now he has the proof, too. Maybe he even set out to test her in that regard ... I wouldn't put it past him. But I wonder why Celeste disappeared. It seems strange to me that she grew tired of Jude so suddenly."

A cryptic smile flitted across Bianca's face. "Well..."

she said, but left the word hanging deliberately and meaningfully between them.

"It seems to me you know something about this?" Tristan said in wonder.

"Could be." Her smile widened.

"Don't tell me.... You *didn't*?"

"What?"

"You didn't ... harm her?"

26

"Excuse me?" Bianca hissed at Tristan. For the moment she seemed to have forgotten that he was her boss. "What do you take me for?" Her brow furrowed intently. "I haven't touched a hair on Celeste's head. I merely made her an offer she couldn't refuse—and I did it only to help *you!*" she added emphatically. "It seems to me that you don't appreciate it, though."

"I ... but of course ... but what exactly did you do?" Tristan looked confused.

Bianca shrugged her shoulders and smiled nonchalantly. "Celeste loves luxury; she likes to spend money for a living, but she's not willing to work for it. And I've made it clear to her that Jude doesn't have what it takes to run the hotel chain successfully. He might be able to give her a great life for a very short time, apart from the fact that he tends to be a bit stingy, as she herself confided in me, but soon he would go broke and she would be the wife of a failure. She wouldn't like that at all. Besides, as soon as we arrived here I noticed how fed up she is with Jude. She absolutely detests him."

"You seem to me to be a very keen observer, my dear Bianca," Tristan said. His tone and facial expression reflected a mixture of awe and shock.

"I guess I am," she replied coquettishly. "And I

offered Celeste an alternative. She's still young and reasonably good-looking. With a nice sum of seed money, she can move in circles where she can land a really fat fish—pardon me, a husband—who really appreciates her."

"And you ... offered her this seed money?" asked Tristan in amazement.

Bianca was smiling triumphantly now. "Mm-hmm."

"But you aren't wealthy ... are you? You wouldn't work as a secretary..."

Bianca made a casual gesture. "Celeste has accepted a down payment, and the prospect of further, very attractive installments, once I'm your associate. The girl has a good nose for business; she sensed right away that she could trust me and that I'm a capable businessperson, unlike her husband."

"Wow." Tristan looked at her as if there were a whole new woman standing in front of him, and not the quiet secretary he knew. But then his brow furrowed.

"Nevertheless," he said, "the down payment you mention must have been pretty handsome. Otherwise I'm sure Celeste wouldn't have given up Jude just like that, even though his prospects may not be particularly rosy in the long run. So what did you pay her? And how did you raise the money?"

"Do you really want to know?"

"Yes...?" He didn't sound convinced.

"I transferred my entire savings to her in one fell swoop. I can say that I already had a small nest egg—after all I work hard, and I also inherited a little. But I will, of course, replenish my account ... for which I have taken a, um, small, inconspicuous loan from your wife. Which I have no intention of paying back."

"You did *what*?" Tristan's eyes were now as big as saucers.

Bianca grinned. Gone was the serious, slightly boring secretary. I was now looking at a two-legged who reminded me of a commander in the military, or rather a spy, who could disguise herself to perfection and make her special abilities available to the highest bidder in every case.

Bianca was clearly a woman who knew exactly what she wanted, and had no qualms about taking unusual and dark paths to achieve it. The perfect murderess, perhaps?

"Don't look so shocked, boss," she said, again in a coquettish tone, "I just relieved your wife of some of her jewels. No woman needs that much bling. And it's in her own best interest, isn't it, if you inherit the hotel chain? Then she won't have to feed you anymore."

"Seriously now?" said Tristan. "Bianca, you ... surprise me." He smiled a little weakly, not seeming to know whether to be afraid or impressed by such boldness.

I, on the other hand, was absolutely certain of one thing: even if he had only promised Bianca a paltry ten percent of his prospective hotel empire, *she* would be the one in charge in no time.

"Are you mad at me?" she asked in an innocent, girlish tone, brushing a strand of hair away from her face.

"If you have concerns..."

"What? No! Don't worry about it! Julia has so much dough, and she's always fobbed me off with just a small allowance. She can buy herself some new jewelry easily!"

"I knew you were going to say that," Bianca replied.

"Oh ... you little demon!" Suddenly and without any warning, Tristan pulled her into his arms—and kissed her passionately.

She resisted for a heartbeat at most, rather for the audience—even if that only consisted of me, the innocent dog—than from genuine shyness, it seemed to me.

"You are such a brilliant woman, Bianca," Tristan whispered after he had released her lips from his again. However, he still held her tightly in his arms, pressing her intimately against him. "I wish you could be more than just my business partner..."

"You womanizer! You can't be serious," Bianca joked, but she too now exuded the unmistakable scent of human desire.

He took her bit of invective personally. In any case, he frowned and pretended to be contrite. "I might have been one in the past—a womanizer, that is. I can't deny that I haven't always been faithful to my wife. But with you, Bianca, it's completely different. You're not like any of the women I've met so far. You are something very special, a gift, do you understand? And I never want to let you go ever again." Again he pressed his lips to hers, and this time his hands also wandered over her body, full of desire.

She moaned softly—which only seemed to spur him on even more.

"Come with me," he whispered in a rough voice. "I've held myself back long enough, so help me God. If my wife is already firmly convinced that you and I are having an affair..."

"...then there's no harm in doing what she's accusing us of anyway?" asked Bianca breathlessly. "But I don't want to be your affair, Tristan, your toy that you throw away afterwards."

"You're not, my dear, not even close. You are so much more. Can't you feel that?"

He kissed her again, his fingers burrowing into her hair, and then he grabbed her hand and pulled her after him. She followed eagerly.

The two of them ran toward the door, almost tripping over me, because they were hardly aware of their surroundings and I didn't get out of the way fast enough. They left the room, hurried along the corridor, and finally disappeared behind Tristan's bedroom door.

I trotted down the hall after them, then stopped in front of the closed door and listened. I could hear someone inside the bedroom pushing something under the handle. A chair? Probably a precautionary measure so that the two were not caught in the act. It was absolutely clear to me what they were up to now.

27

I settled down in front of Tristan's bedroom door and pondered the meaning of the two-leggeds' lovemaking—apart from the obvious, of course.

What I had just observed and overheard had strengthened my impression that Tristan and Bianca had *not* actually had an affair until now—that they were all over each other for the first time. In other words, I now had confirmation that the false detective must have definitely faked the evidence of Tristan's infidelity, which he had duly presented to Julia.

But was the attack on Julia—and the threats against Victoria and the pipsqueak—still about this first murder case? Or did the death of Edward Laymon have nothing to do with the danger his client now seemed to be facing?

I must have dozed off while pondering these questions, because suddenly loud caterwauling from the ground floor woke me from a deep sleep.

Pearl.

It took me a moment before I realized where I was—in front of Tristan's bedroom! Through the door I could still hear muffled moans and whispers. Apparently Bianca and Tristan were planning on having fun together all night.

"Athos, where are you?" Pearl squeaked from somewhere on the ground floor, so miserably that I tripped over my own paws in shock as I tried to sprint off to her aid.

I made it to the stairs, staggering and still half dazed from sleep, rolling down them more than running, and luckily not breaking my neck. A thick coat definitely has its advantages.

When I landed, I noticed that there was a commotion in the hallway outside Julia's bedroom. Victoria was running through the door and turning on the light, and Julia's and André's voices were coming from inside the room. Both seemed to be beside themselves with panic.

Pearl came galloping toward me in the hallway. "Where have you been, Athos? Are you all right? Didn't you hear Julia scream? I woke Victoria up right away and directed her here," she announced to me proudly. "But you were gone."

"I was shadowing Bianca and Tristan," I defended myself. "They really are having an affair with each other, after all. They're having sex right now."

"What, that can't be..."

"Take my word for it."

"Then I must have ... misunderstood something. Come on, let's hear what the humans are talking about. Julia has been attacked again! And not in a subtle way this time."

Oh no. And I hadn't noticed a thing—what kind of

watchdog was I, anyway?

I quickly followed the tiny one into Julia's bedroom.

The actress, who was as white as her fluffy down comforter, was sitting upright in bed, her mouth gaping open and closing as if she could hardly breathe, and a stream of tears running down her cheeks. She clung to Victoria, who had just joined her at the bedside.

To the left of her, on the floor in front of the chair where he had been sitting, André knelt with his head in both hands.

"Damn, what is ... wrong with me? I think ... I've been drugged," he moaned with a heavy clicking of his tongue. "A sleeping draught?" He shook his head frantically, probably in an effort to shake himself awake, but that only seemed to give him another dizzy spell.

"Call an ambulance ... please, Victoria," he managed, as if each syllable were costing him his last bit of strength. "And the Inspector! Julia's been attacked again!"

Victoria didn't need to be told twice; she reached for the nightstand, where Julia's cell phone still lay, held the device in front of the actress's face to unlock it, and was connected to 911 in no time. "We need an ambulance, quickly." She glanced at Julia, but seemed unable to discern what exactly was wrong with her. What the attacker, of whom there was no trace, had done to her.

She gave the name of the hotel and the number of Julia's villa. "Please also inform the police," she added.

"Chief Inspector Nüring. There has been a new attack." She remained purposely vague.

As soon as she'd hung up, she turned to André. "What exactly happened?" she asked him breathlessly.

Julia was still sobbing so hard that Victoria couldn't get a sensible word out of her. She howled and panted and was completely beside herself. Victoria stroked her hair to calm her down, but at first it didn't seem to help.

The actress didn't even seem to notice when Pearl jumped onto the bed to comfort her. I briefly considered shock therapy—a soaking-wet tongue in the middle of the face—but then decided against it. It helped with Pearl, but Victoria would probably not appreciate such measures with a two-legged in her care.

"I ... I feel so dizzy," André complained. He shook himself like a dog that has just had a bath, in a renewed attempt to get rid of his drowsiness. "I was sleeping ... like a rock, but then suddenly there was a noise. A scream ... Julia. She jerked me out of sleep, I tried to get to my feet, but then I fell. Everything was spinning. But I saw ... a shadow running away from her, out of the room. The inspector must arrest him. He tried to kill Julia!"

"Who is *he*?" asked Victoria, but she seemed to guess the answer before André spoke it. "Tristan?"

"No!" Julia howled. "Not him—not my Tristan! That witch must have driven him to it!"

"You screamed his name, Julia," said the nurse.

The actress suddenly clawed her hands through Pearl's fur, so that the poor pipsqueak howled with fright. Victoria came to her rescue.

"You're hurting her," she said softly, as she released Julia's cramped fingers and allowed Pearl to slip away.

Julia slapped her hands to her face and was shaken by a new, violent crying fit.

"What did you hear? And see?" Victoria turned back to André, who had now managed to pull himself up off the floor at the opposite edge of the bed and fall onto the free side of the mattress, breathing heavily. He lay there curled up, massaging his temples with his hands.

"The shadow ... the attacker, he bent over Julia ... and pressed a pillow onto her face," he managed to say.

He pointed to a small white cushion that was lying seemingly quite innocently beside Julia's head. "She must have somehow managed to fight back, and caught her breath after all, and screamed his name. That jolted me out of my sleep; I tried to rush to her aid. But I felt very dizzy, and I fell off the chair instead of getting to my feet ... but at least he let go of her and rushed out of the room."

"Is that true?" Victoria turned to Julia, who was still crying but had now at least lowered her hands to her chest. "You were able to recognize him? Your husband? Did you manage to see his face before he put the pillow..." She broke off. "It was dark in the room, wasn't it?"

"I couldn't see anything," Julia replied tonelessly.

"When I came to, he was already pressing the pillow to my face. I thought I was going to suffocate. But he—he said, '*Goodbye, dear heart. Till death do us part. You'll never bully me again*! But I've never bullied him. I mean, how could he do that to me? I'm telling you, that snake put him up to it! Completely bewitched him because she wants him for herself! She's the guilty one."

"I can't believe she's still defending him." Pearl now pushed her way into my field of vision and stared up at me from her baby blue eyes. "She's really fallen for this killer completely! It's crazy."

"She loves him," I pointed out.

"Crazy, as I said."

"Tristan calls you *dear heart*?" said Victoria, more to herself than to Julia. "And *till death do us part,* I suppose only a husband would say that. I'm afraid there's really no doubt about it; it was he who tried to kill you, Julia." She glanced at the door, as if to assure herself that there was no more danger from that quarter.

"It was him," André confirmed. "He says *dear heart* quite often, usually when he's about to tell Julia some disgusting lie the next moment," he added bitterly. "I could only dimly make him out, but the outline matched him. Height, general shape.... You didn't run into him out in the hall?"

"No," Victoria said. "I guess it took me a moment too long to find my way out of bed and run over here. Pearl woke me up, but I didn't realize what she wanted me to do at first..."

"I used your method to get her awake, Athos," the tiny one explained to me proudly. "Worked just fine, and isn't as brutal as using the claws."

"Tongue in ear?" I asked.

"Exactly."

"How considerate of you—much better than claws indeed."

"Where is the ambulance?" André asked abruptly. He stared at Victoria as if she must know the answer. Then he bent down, grasping hold of Julia's right hand. "It's going to be okay," he murmured. "You're safe now."

And turning to Victoria again, he said, "I could swear I was given a sleeping draught—both of us, maybe. And Julia, too, to make her defenseless. I ... am still all woozy. He wanted to make sure he'd have an easy time with us."

Victoria suddenly turned pale. A realization seemed to have come to her at André's words.

"I think we have all been drugged!" she blurted out. "A sleeping draught, yes. The Chief Inspector could hardly stand on his feet with tiredness when he left me, too, and I myself..."

She ran her hand over her forehead. "The hot chocolate, that must have been it! They put something in it—drugging me and the Inspector as well. Bianca brought it to us ... and to you, too?"

"We each had a cup," André confirmed. "Julia and I—it was I who ordered the hot chocolate from room service. I came up with the idea because I wanted to do something good for all of us. A nightcap, just the thing after this crazy day, I thought."

"Who opened the front door when room service came by?" Victoria prompted him.

"That was me, too. I took the cups through to the kitchen, but then my cell phone beeped. It was a message from Julia, who needed help in the bathroom. I went to her and asked Bianca, whom I met on the way, to distribute the cups to everyone for me."

"You didn't take any with you? For Julia or for yourself?" asked Victoria.

He shook his head. "I ... I should have, but I was distracted. Julia doesn't like to wait when she needs something."

"Am I really that awful?" Julia suddenly exclaimed. "Do I bully you too, like Tristan said?"

"What? No, for heaven's sake! That's really not what I meant to say! I'm your nurse, and you can't do a lot of things by yourself. So it's only natural that you would call for me. I really don't blame you for that." It wouldn't have taken much for him to have hugged Julia.

She sniffled.

Outside, the siren of a police car, or perhaps the ambulance, was clearly heard.

And at that moment Tristan entered the room. He was wearing a silk robe and his cheeks were flushed. I knew exactly why.

"What's going on?" he asked, seemingly taken aback. "I was going to the bathroom—and I heard voices."

Julia cried out, startled. Victoria and André jumped up from the bed at the same time; both seemed fully awake now and ready to defend Julia.

I didn't miss the chance to get onto my paws with a giant leap—and I reached Tristan first. Snarling, I put myself into his path. "Not one step further," I growled.

But while I was acting like a killer wolf in front of him, a thought spread through my head: Tristan had been in bed with Bianca. How could he have sneaked into his wife's room at the same time to smother Julia with a pillow?

28

Tristan Harrington was arrested. Two police officers, who'd arrived together with the ambulance and before Chief Inspector Nüring, handcuffed him and took him away after Victoria had described to them what had happened.

He protested loudly against his arrest. Again and again he affirmed that he had been fast asleep and had not even been near his wife's bedroom.

But the statements of Victoria, followed by André's and Julia's, probably spoke all too clearly in the eyes of the officers. Tristan was loaded into the police car and the two constables drove away with him as soon as Chief Inspector Nüring arrived.

The rest of us had all gathered together in Julia's room. Bianca also joined us; she was wearing a robe and biting her nails, but she didn't utter a word the whole time. Julia stared at her venomously when she wasn't trembling and clinging to Victoria, shaken by a new crying fit.

It was only when the Chief Inspector began to have a brief one-on-one conversation with each of those present that Bianca seemed to come to the decision that she should defend Tristan.

Pearl and I, of course, followed the Inspector into the living room he was using for his questioning and listened intently to what Bianca had to say.

"Mr. Harrington could not have assaulted his wife," she said in a formal and very composed tone. "He and I, um, we were working. In his office. We had just gone to sleep when not two minutes later the commotion started downstairs. So the timing can't be right. Tristan—I mean Mr. Harrington—is innocent."

"You were working?" the Inspector asked skeptically. "At half past one in the morning?"

"Yeah ... it's not that unusual. Mr. Harrington is, um, a bit of a night owl, you know. And so am I."

She was lying—and she wasn't very good at it. But I understood that she didn't want to confess the whole truth to the Chief Inspector, that she and Tristan hadn't actually been in the study at the time in question, but had been enjoying themselves in his bed.

The Chief Inspector might have suspected this; he had already been led to believe that Bianca and Tristan were having an affair, based on the allegations of Edward Laymon and his faked photos.

At Bianca's statement, he now frowned skeptically and said, "Please accompany me to the station, Ms. Fleming. I have more questions for you."

"Am I under arrest?" cried Bianca, startled. "I swear to you, it's the truth! I..."

"You are not under arrest, Ms. Fleming, at least not yet. But I'll tell you frankly what I think: you planned the attacks on Mrs. Trapp together with Mr. Harrington. He may have carried them out alone, but you knew about them."

"No, that's not true! Neither one of us planned anything!"

"And you didn't kill Edward Laymon either? Maybe because he tried to blackmail you with the knowledge of your secret affair?"

"What? No, for God's sake! I want a lawyer!"

"You're free to do that, of course. But now please come with me."

He stood up. Bianca protested a few more times, but finally she complied and followed the Inspector out of the room.

He said goodbye to Victoria, with the words, "We'll talk later, okay? We'll have to take your statement down at the station too, but get some sleep first. It's not that urgent."

He stroked my head, bent down and caressed Pearl, then left the house with Bianca.

Victoria, Pearl and I returned to Julia's bedroom.

The paramedics from the rescue team were arguing with the actress. They wanted to take Julia to the hospital for some check-ups, but she affirmed that there was nothing wrong with her and insisted on staying at the hotel.

"I'm no longer in any danger here," she said bitterly. Her eyes were so red by now that I was reminded of a vampire who fed on nothing but blood.

An unfavorable comparison, admittedly; I really pitied the poor woman. How must it feel when the one you loved most in the world was secretly plotting your murder?

On the other paw, I just couldn't get rid of the thought that had been raging through my head the whole time: Tristan *couldn't* have committed the attack on Julia, I was convinced of that. He had been safely in his room, having a night of fun with Bianca. It was also a heinous betrayal of his wife, but not to the same extent as a murderous plot.

The paramedics gave up trying to persuade Julia and moved away.

"I can still feel his hands in the small of my back from that time on the balcony—at the Black Cliffs Hotel. It's like it was yesterday," Julia told Victoria as André escorted the two paramedics to the door. "The way I can still feel the pillow on my face." She gently touched her cheeks.

"You can remember what happened now? Completely?" asked Victoria.

"Not completely ... no, not that. But I'm quite sure now that he pushed me, that I didn't jump or fall by myself. Why on earth, Victoria? Why does he hate me so? Why did he detest me so much even then?"

She probably didn't expect an answer to that question, because in the next breath she said, "Go home and get some sleep, Victoria. I thank you for your assistance, but now ... I want to be alone."

Victoria nodded. "You're welcome to call me tomorrow or the next day if you want to talk. Anytime, okay?"

"Thank you, you are really very kind. I would be happy to see you again—and your little ones, too." Pearl, sitting next to her, received a tender pat.

"They are so adorable, your little fur babies," she said with a sorrowful expression. "Maybe I should get some pets, too. Their love is unconditional, isn't it?"

"It is," Victoria confirmed. "I'm not sure I trust anyone as much as I trust my Athos."

I grew a few inches on the spot.

"Cats, after all, are rather whimsical in nature," she added with a smile as she looked down at Pearl, "but they love us in their own way, too, I'm sure."

"Whimsical? Me?" protested Pearl immediately. "Pah. *Independent*, that's what we cats are. That's all! Not as doggishly devoted as *some*."

"Hey, don't get cocky!" I admonished her.

"Try to get some more sleep," André said to Julia, "and I'll lie down in my room for a while. This sleeping draught we were all given..."

"You seriously think I could manage to sleep now?" Julia asked, interrupting him. New tears shimmered in the corners of her eyes, but she impatiently wiped them away. "I don't know if I'll ever be able to sleep again ... or if I want to sleep forever. Without Tristan..."

"You mustn't say that!" André cried. He reached for her hand, squeezing it tightly. "Don't even think it! Life goes on. You still have so many beautiful and amazing things ahead of you, I'm sure. Many happy years."

Julia tried to smile, but failed. The corners of her

mouth twitched, but the next moment she was already fighting new tears. It was impossible not to notice. By now the room smelled like a cemetery; grief had enveloped us in a dark, malodorous cloud.

Victoria drove home with Pearl and me, and fell exhausted on the sofa. She was probably still too wired to sleep, but she put her feet up, massaged her temples and cuddled a bit with Pearl. Of course, that didn't stop my detective colleague from discussing the case with me at the same time.

"You must have been mistaken, Athos," she insisted between purrs directed at Victoria. "As for Tristan and Bianca's alibi, maybe they just had sex for a minute—a quickie, as the bipeds call it—and then ran down to the first floor to murder Julia."

"Quite an unusual program, don't you think?" I grumbled. "Sex and then murder?"

"I keep telling you, the humans are *weird*."

"But I was outside the door of Tristan's bedroom," I protested again. "And the two of them didn't get past me."

"Maybe you were sound asleep."

"It's not like my name is Pearl and I would sleep through the end of the world."

Pearl's whiskers twitched, but fortunately she did not immediately extend her claws and swat at me. On the contrary, she seemed to believe what I had stated.

"Then Julia was wrong about her attacker?" she said

after a brief pause. "And so was André, who saw Tristan fleeing the room?"

"Yes…"

"But there was no one else in the house, was there?" said Pearl. "Steven and Jude are staying in the mansion next door. I'm sure we would have noticed if they had come over."

"They didn't," I said. "When we left Julia's house earlier on with Victoria, I looked over by the other villa. The snow cover there was untouched. No one had left or entered their house in the last few hours."

"And what if Celeste or Scarlett didn't leave after all, and were just hiding, and sneaked into Julia's mansion?" suggested Pearl. "They could have gotten a key card sometime during the day, hid somewhere in the house, and then struck in the night."

"Well honestly, that sounds very far-fetched, too," I objected. "And what motive would any of them have to murder Julia?"

"No one has a motive to hurt her except Tristan," Pearl said, "because he'd inherit a lot of money. And be free for his new girlfriend—for Bianca. Even though I don't think he's that eager to marry her."

"But he couldn't have been the attacker who put a pillow on Julia's face," I insisted. "And neither could Bianca."

"Then both Julia and André must have lied to us," Pearl concluded. "That's the only alternative we have left. But it doesn't make sense, does it?"

"The child," I said, "that boy … where did he go? Was

he possibly still hidden somewhere in the house?"

Pearl looked at me in disbelief. "And then he crept into Julia's room late at night to put a pillow on her face? After mixing sleeping drugs in all the other humans' cocoa beforehand? You can't be serious."

"If the boy stabbed the detective, he may also have tried to suffocate Julia," I insisted. "You said small doesn't necessarily mean harmless. Remember? And maybe he's just severely deranged."

"We have to get back to Julia," Pearl decided. "If Tristan really is innocent, then her life is still in danger."

"André is with her," I reminded Pearl—even if he would hardly be on guard now.

"Maybe *he's* the problem!" exclaimed Pearl suddenly. "He's the only one we haven't suspected yet. He could easily have poisoned Julia's orange juice or put a pillow on her face."

"But he was the one who raised the alarm," I protested. "The one who saved her life, during the first attack with the antihypertensive."

Pearl mewled in frustration. "Yeah, that's right. *Grrr*. We've got to get to her, Athos. She's in danger, and besides, we have to prove Tristan's innocence if you're right about his alibi. Our work isn't done yet!"

That was true, of course. We couldn't allow anything to happen to Julia after all that we'd been through, or permit an innocent Tristan to end up behind bars. And possibly Bianca, too.

29

"Okay, I'll bark Victoria awake," I said. Our two-legged had fallen asleep on the sofa in the meantime, even though she had assumed earlier that she was too agitated to do so. Pearl's purring was at least as effective as any sleeping draught.

I didn't hesitate for long, but instead yelped loudly, and lapped at Victoria's hand. This was not as effective as the tongue-in-ear method, but it was sufficient for my current purposes.

Victoria arose from her sleep with a groan and looked at me as if she had never seen a dog in her life.

She swallowed a few times and rubbed her eyes until she realized where she was and who she was looking at. "Athos ... what's going on? What the hell kind of noise are you making?"

She glanced toward the window, probably to make quite sure it wasn't yet time to get up. I wasn't wearing a watch, naturally, but estimated that it must be four or five in the morning at the most. Sunrise was still a long time coming, and the blizzard had abated only a little. The howling of the wind could still be heard, and thick white flakes continued to rage through the darkness.

"Come on, you have to get up. We must check on Julia!" I urged Victoria. "She might still be in danger!"

Or she had been playing a trick on all of us to put her faithless husband behind bars—the thought hadn't occurred to me until now. Was Julia trying to frame him for attempted murder as punishment for his infidelity?

Could it be true? In any event, we had to get back to the Harrington Hotel!

"You want out now, Athos?" moaned Victoria. "Are you serious? What a time to go for a walk."

She rubbed her eyes again, then put on a sympathetic smile. "It's okay, sweetie, I guess I can't blame you. We've all been through a lot. No wonder you can't seem to settle down."

"I *am* calm," I protested. "But we have to get to Julia—not take me for a walk! I don't have the bladder of a Chihuahua!"

Victoria shuffled into the foyer, put on a jacket at the coat rack, then opened the front door.

Pearl and I stormed out and ran straight to the car parked in the front yard. This way we could hopefully make it clear to Victoria that we didn't have a nighttime stroll in mind.

Victoria followed us drowsily, but didn't seem to realize what we were trying to tell her. I straightened up at the driver's door, braced my paws against the side window of the car, and panted encouragingly at her. "Come on, get in the car, Victoria. Come on! There's no time to lose!"

She did nothing of the sort. "What's this all about?" she grumbled instead. "You really need to calm down,

Athos! You're going to scratch my paint. Come on, get down."

Oh man, the two-leggeds and their cars. They are like sacred cows to them.

I ran away from the car and then toward it again. It usually helps when I use this method—towards the target, away from the target, and towards it again.

But this time Victoria seemed hopelessly slow on the uptake. She looked as if she might fall asleep standing up at any moment, despite the cold that made her shiver and shake.

She turned and walked back toward the house. "Okay, walk finished," she announced.

For a moment, I considered just running off. But that was not a good plan; Victoria wouldn't just go to sleep if Pearl and I disappeared at random into the driving snow. She would worry, try to follow us—and probably freeze to death herself. She had no fur, and she wore only an inadequate jacket and shoes that were more suitable for a cozy autumn day than for an arctic expedition.

Reluctantly I followed her into the house, and Pearl scurried after me. She'd been sinking almost up to her neck in the snow, although she'd tried to run in my paw prints.

Inside she shook herself violently, looking so disgusted it was almost comical. "Nasty stuff, this snow!" she hissed.

Poor little sofa cat.

But to my astonishment, she immediately announced, "Okay, we need a plan B. Good thing I'm a top strategist—I'll explain everything in a minute."

"A what?" I repeated incredulously.

Victoria was about to lock the front door behind us, but Pearl suddenly screamed and howled at the top of her lungs, and in the next moment had rushed up the stairs to the upper floor as if pursued by a pack of bloodhounds.

Victoria whirled around and ran after her. "Pearl? Oh God, what's wrong? Are you hurt?"

I followed after the two of them. What had the tiny one cooked up this time?

Once upstairs, we found Pearl on Victoria's bed, where she continued to cry and meow like there was no tomorrow. Victoria sat with her, examined her to see if she was hurt, and finally started petting her to calm her down.

But of course Pearl wasn't hurt; she was just putting on a show.

She didn't have to explain to me what her plan actually was, because when she climbed onto Victoria's belly and held our human in bed that way, her plan dawned on me.

In all the excitement, Victoria had forgotten to lock the front door—and now she was being cuddled by Pearl and would surely fall asleep as soon as the kitten had apparently calmed down. Running downstairs once more to lock up—she would forget all about that. And that's exactly what the little schemer, who was now already breathing calmly and evenly again, was speculating on. "Sleep well, Victoria," she murmured happily to herself.

Pearl really was up to every trick. As if to confirm my thoughts, she now intoned a soothing purr, and I could see that Victoria's eyes were already falling shut.

"Clever plan," I had to admit. "We can take off as soon as she falls asleep, and she won't even notice. I can open the front door no problem, as long as it's unlocked. But you do realize that it's quite a walk to Julia's hotel? That we have to trudge through the snow, and that it's sub-zero outside?"

"We have no other choice," Pearl replied bravely. "Besides, I am a descendant of the proud forest cats of Russia," she added, with a deadly serious face. The little beast was making fun of me, just because I occasionally talked about *my* ancestors, the proud wolves of Alaska. But really only very rarely.

We set off on our way. Fortunately, I knew approximately where the Harrington Hotel was from where we were staying. We had already driven the distance by car, and I liked to look out the window instead of just taking a nap.

I went ahead and Pearl walked behind me in my slipstream, and to pass the time we continued to speculate about who really wanted to kill Julia—or whether she had fooled us all in the end.

There were so many unanswered questions. Why did Edward Laymon have to die? Who had written the anonymous letters to Julia? And what about the strange little boy?

Admittedly it was quite frosty out here, even for me in my thick coat of fur. Storm, snow and the cold of the night were a challenging combination. Nasty, as the tiny one would say, especially when you had to cover a longer distance.

I squinted back over my shoulder at Pearl, who looked like a yeti, so much of her fur being already covered with snow.

But she didn't speak a word of complaint. She was clearly in her Hero Mode. She was "going to save the world now." She would not back down, even if she froze her tiny butt off.

But that could not be allowed to happen. I stopped, and she almost ran into me—probably because she had narrowed her eyes into very small slits.

"Athos!" she mewed. "What's wrong?"

"Would you like to climb on my back?" I suggested casually. She mustn't notice that I felt sorry for her, otherwise she would want to prove to me, stubborn as she was, that she could be a true outdoor cat.

Following some inspiration, I added, "You know, like people do with horses. I can carry you—I wouldn't mind your weight. And we would make faster progress. The sooner we reach Julia, the better."

She hesitated, but not for very long. I dropped onto my stomach and she climbed nimbly onto my back.

I could feel her little body trembling. My idea to offer her a ride had come not a moment too soon. She clawed her way into my fur, snuggled up close to me, and I trotted off. Over-excited as I was, I almost tried a

neigh.
What a crazy night.

30

On our way to the hotel, we were already beginning to see the first motorists on the roads. So despite the continuing darkness, the night would soon give way to day, but it was so cold and so dark that it was hard to imagine ever seeing the sun again.

Quite exhausted, but with a cat on my back who was no longer shaking, I arrived in front of Julia's villa. Everything seemed to be quiet in the house; now we just had to get inside.

Oh well, sometimes the direct way is the best one. I just barked and scratched the front door with my paw. Someone would open, hopefully, André or Julia herself....

They would be surprised to see us here, in the middle of the night in this snowy expanse, but hopefully not deny us entry.

Fortunately, that's exactly what happened. André opened the door for us, in a good mood, but was startled when he saw us. "Wow, it's you two? Where did you come from? Where is your mistress? It's a wonder you haven't frozen to death."

He willingly stepped aside, and I trotted into the house with my little rider still on my back. I made quite a mess in the hallway shaking the snow out of my coat after Pearl had climbed off me, but André didn't hold it against me.

Pearl marched straight to the kitchen. "Now I'm willing to eat anything," she said, "even sausage."

André was actually kind enough to raid the refrigerator for her. There wasn't much, and it was probably too early for room service, but for once Pearl didn't complain and ate what he put in front of her.

"I'll send your mistress a message that you're here," he said, already typing away on his cell phone the next moment.

I assumed that the beeping that announced a new message would not wake Victoria, even if she hadn't switched her phone to silent. She usually did that at night.

Pearl and I wanted to hold the fort here with Julia, to finally find out what was really going on in the actress's villa—and to hopefully unmask the real assassin. We didn't need Victoria coming to pick us up anytime soon.

After the small snack in the kitchen, we followed André to Julia's bedroom. She was awake, holding a big cup of coffee in both hands and very happy to see us.

"Did you escape, you two?" she asked. "Just to visit me? You guys are so cute!" She reached out her arms to me, bent over and rested her head on mine. Then she turned to Pearl, who hopped up on the bed with her.

"What a bummer," the tiny one commented. "It looks like everything is just fine here. Did we make a mistake, Athos? André certainly doesn't seem to be after Julia's life—nor does anyone else. Now that she's protected only by her caregiver, an assassin would have a golden opportunity to strike again, and this time for good."

"I just don't know," I grumbled.

"Wouldn't you like to try to get some sleep, dear?" André said to Julia. "I'm sure it would do you good."

He sat down on the free side of the bed and looked anxiously at the actress. There was great tenderness in his gaze.

"I can't," Julia replied. Her voice sounded rough as sandpaper. "I won't—never again."

"Be reasonable, darling."

"But I don't want to be reasonable. I just lost my husband! And by the way, I think it's inappropriate for you to call me *darling*," she snapped at him abruptly. "You may be well-intentioned, but I can't hear it now."

"Wow. Sorry about that." He furrowed his brow.

She looked at him inquiringly.

He stared back.

Something strange was suddenly in the air. André suddenly began to give off that smell that I had detected only a few hours previously in Tristan's and his secretary's office. The unmistakable scent of human desire.

What did it mean?

He continued to stare at his employer, although I didn't know exactly how to interpret his gaze. More serious, at any rate, than just a moment before, and almost angry? But also full of that desire that was becoming increasingly clear in my nose.

When he began to speak again, his voice sounded changed. "I can't believe you're shedding a tear for that bastard, Julia," he said slowly, emphasizing each word. "He cheated on you. Certainly not only with Bianca. He wanted to kill you, damn it! All he ever cared about was your money."

"Shut up. I don't want to hear it!" she said sharply. A wrinkle of anger had formed on her forehead, a deep furrow of sorrow and anguish.

"You have to hear it, dear," he insisted. His voice swelled. "You have to finally realize how blind you've been. Always Tristan, Tristan, Tristan. You were so infatuated with him, so blinded, that you never realized who truly loved you."

"Excuse me?" she snapped. The frown line had disappeared and given way to an expression of astonishment.

He suddenly leaned over to her, so abruptly that Pearl scurried away, startled. He stretched out his arms, wrapped them around Julia's upper body, and pulled her to him. Then he kissed her with a passion that took my breath away.

Pearl let out a startled meow.

Julia, however, didn't fancy this outburst of tenderness in the slightest. She stiffened and pushed her nurse away from her, with more force than I would have thought her capable of and with less than romantic words. "Are you crazy, André? How dare you!"

She slapped him hard across the face, causing him to groan and recoil. Then she ran the back of her hand over her lips as if to remove something disgusting from them.

"How dare you!" she hissed again. Her anger seemed to increase. "I should fire you for that!" she added.

"*Fire* me?" he repeated. Fury now flared in his voice—and also in his gaze.

He grabbed her arms so tightly that she couldn't get away from him. "Look at me, Julia! And tell me that you don't love me. You and I are meant for each other, won't you finally realize that? I've been serving you like a slave for years, doing everything for you, taking care of you, comforting you, being there for you ... and you can't do anything but cry after that bastard? Now that we're finally rid of him...?"

He tried to kiss her again. "Julia. My darling—" he murmured.

This time she couldn't hit him, because he still held both of her arms, but she braced herself against him with all her strength.

"Stop it!" she screeched. "Let go of me right now, you maniac! I'll scream!"

I pushed my head forward and growled at André. What the hell was he doing? Had he lost his mind?

He let go of Julia, but his gaze remained fixed on her lips. There was something in his eyes that made me think of a wounded predator, and they are known to be dangerous. Unpredictable.

Julia stared at him as if she saw a complete stranger

in front of her—a man she was suddenly afraid of. I could smell it clearly, as clearly as André's scent signaled to me that he was crazy about this woman. That he desired her with every fiber of his body.

"Oh, dear fried fish," Pearl hissed from beside me. "This isn't good."

"You can say that again," I returned through bared teeth. I didn't take my eyes off André.

And what did he do? He suddenly had a jackknife in his hand, which he snapped open.

Now it was I who had to back away. A blade of sharp sparkling steel was a convincing argument.

"André!" Julia cried in horror. "Oh God, what are you doing? Put the knife away."

He did nothing of the sort. He kept the knife in his hand, and stayed alert and very tense.

But at least he didn't go after Julia or me. He leaned his back against the head of the bed, but didn't take his eyes off Julia.

There was still a great tenderness in the look he gave her, which he now emphasized with his words: "I love you, Julia. I always have, and I won't deny it now. Never again. You'll see what you have in me, and you'll realize that you return my feelings. That we are meant for each other—"

Julia clawed her hands into the covers. "You're insane," she whispered. "Completely out of your mind."

This was clearly not the answer André had hoped for.

"Oh really, do you think so?" he replied coldly. The tenderness that had been in his gaze a moment ago vanished. "So ungrateful," he whispered. "After all I've done for you."

31

Julia stared at her nurse with wide eyes. "What exactly do you mean ... *done for me*?" she whispered. Her voice quivered.

"You ask me that? I got rid of the man who's been taking advantage of you for all these years."

Pearl and I were not the only ones to notice that André no longer talked about Tristan wanting to murder Julia. She probably hadn't missed it either.

"André," she said in a rough voice, "was it really Tristan who ... attacked me? You're scaring me."

He laughed harshly. "He may not have wanted to kill you, but it was obvious he treated you like dirt! Don't you see that? Isn't that enough for you? He had to go, that pig! Behind bars where he belongs!"

"You're saying ... oh God, what did you do? *Set* him *up*? Framed him for the attacks on me, to get him arrested?"

André said nothing, but he didn't shake his head either. He just stared at her longingly, but at the same time with growing fury.

She didn't even seem to notice, she was so wound up. Her whole focus was on understanding what had happened to her. I must admit that I myself was dizzy from what was taking place before my eyes. From the abominable truth, which Julia was putting together herself so agonizingly, piece by piece.

She kept talking, trying to understand what exactly had befallen her, what exactly André had done, the good, dear nurse-companion who had suddenly turned into a dangerous maniac.

"If Tristan ... didn't attack me," she stammered, "then who did?" Her voice failed. She swallowed, cleared her throat. "Was it you who ... tried to kill me, André?"

"I would never hurt you, dear," he said coldly. "You haven't been in mortal danger for a second these past few days. I just wanted you to be mine at last. I couldn't wait any longer, surely you understand? No more watching your cursed husband trample all over your feelings, while you still couldn't let go of him. If I hadn't finally gotten rid of him, I would have remained invisible to you forever. Just the nice nurse who sacrificed himself for you."

"Not in danger for a second?" she repeated. "...in the last few days. What's that supposed to mean? You were ... wait, you were just *pretending* someone was trying to kill me? But then ... I don't understand. My memory ... what happened at the Black Cliffs Hotel? I was in more than mortal danger there. But I didn't even know you back then."

André clicked his tongue moodily. "Ah, you knew me alright. You just forgot all about me. After your *accident*."

"My accident? But it wasn't a..." She expelled her breath, startled. "Who the hell are you, André?"

"Your most ardent fan, my dear. Always have been.

The man who will love you for the rest of your life. Who will never look at another, I swear to you."

I could see how the fur on the back of Pearl's neck stood on end next to me, and I didn't feel any different. I had expected everything, but not this. André, a crazed fan? A stalker? But I still didn't understand what exactly he had done.

Julia was groping in the dark just as we were. She pressed her back against the headboard; if she had been able to move her legs, she would have left the bed long ago. I saw her squint at her cell phone, but unfortunately it was now on a dresser perhaps two dog lengths from the bed. I could have brought it to her, no problem, but André would certainly not have stood idly by while she called the police.

Julia kept talking—she was afraid, but she also wanted to understand what had happened to her. You could see that in her face.

"So you're behind all the attacks on me, André?" she mused to herself in a hoarse voice. "And behind the letters, too, perhaps? You set me up; you wanted me to see Tristan as a murderer. No, more than that, you wanted to put him behind bars."

"Just so we can finally be together, dear," he replied. And he even smiled as he said it.

"But I ... remembered," she said. "I didn't try to commit suicide back at the Black Cliffs Hotel, I was pushed. I can feel the hands in my back quite clearly, the memory will probably stay with me forever now. Then you were ... in that hotel too? On my balcony?

And you pushed me? Not Tristan—*you* wanted to kill me!"

"How can you think that! I would never harm a hair on your head," André cried indignantly. "I adored you, Julia, at first as just a fan. That's why I came to the hotel, to meet you. And you were nice to me—very nice, in fact. You liked me, and showed me that very clearly. At least, that's what I thought. You invited me up to your room. We drank cocktails on your balcony that evening. But in reality you were just playing with me, to make your husband jealous. That's what you confessed to me when I wanted to kiss you, when I declared my love to you, just like today. You pushed me away. And I got so angry. I didn't want to hurt you, but you spurned me, called me mad, just when I'd revealed my heart to you. Just like you're doing now. You've learned nothing, my dear. And are you surprised when a man goes berserk?"

"You pushed me off that accursed balcony! You wanted to kill me!" Julia screamed.

"It was an accident! You were as unruly then as you are now, and you trampled on my feelings! You looked at me like some disgusting insect, pushed me away from you, and that's when I..." He groaned and stared at Julia with a pleading expression. "I lost my temper, just for a tiny moment. I pushed you back when you turned away from me. Not that hard..."

"Oh my God ... not that hard? You pushed me over the railing and into the abyss. It was *your* hands in my back that I remembered!"

"Darling ... please forgive me! I told you I didn't mean to hurt you. I swear to you! And I've done penance for that stupid, terrible misfortune. All these years! Fortunately I was already a nurse by profession at that time, and I was able to apply to you when you ended up in the hospital—paraplegic and without any memory."

A single tear ran down his cheek. "Oh, my poor angel ... I truly didn't want to harm you," he affirmed again. "I wanted to do everything I could to make it up to you. I applied for the job as your nurse, and I asked for a very small salary, even though I had the best references. You know that, don't you? And I've served you all these years, caring for you and pampering you, proving my love for you. Now you must see it at last, Julia."

"Or what?" she croaked.

He smiled frostily at her, with more than a spark of madness in his gaze.

"I won't be rejected again, Julia," he said slowly, but in a tone that made me go cold. His voice still sounded insanely tender, and yet now an open threat resonated in it.

"Do something, Athos," I heard Pearl mewl beside me. "You've got to stop him!"

She was right; I could no longer just watch.

He no longer held the knife in his hand, in order to fight. It lay next to him, ready to hand on the bed. I had to be quick before he could reach for it.

I tensed my body, wishing for a brief desperate moment that I were a husky after all, for once. Smaller, lighter, more agile and much faster than a Malamute.

I started to jump up, but then I stopped. I would land on Julia if I pushed off from the ground here. She was between me and André, and not even a husky could have jumped over her to knock out her caregiver. It would have taken a kangaroo to do that.

I had to circle the bed, and approach André from the other side. And I had to do it without him realizing right away what I was up to and grabbing the knife. Otherwise I had no chance whatsoever.

I was a big, strong dog, but he in turn was a big, strong man. Twice as heavy as me, and armed to boot. A serious opponent if I didn't have the element of surprise on my side. And I had probably lost that advantage; he was on guard, his gaze following me as I circled the bed as casually as I could.

When I reached his side of the bed and finally prepared to pounce on him, he caught me cold. He didn't grab the knife as I had feared, but he suddenly jumped up before I could do so and sped toward me. Before I knew what was happening, he'd grabbed me and lifted me up like a puppy.

I yelped in fright, squirming in his arms to get free, and tried to snap at him, but he had a firm grip on me. He ran the few steps to the door and threw me out in a high arc.

I just managed to maneuver my legs under my body and thus spare myself a complete crash landing. But I was not fast enough to run back into the room; André slammed the door in my face. And then he did what Tristan had done a few hours earlier—he wedged a chair under the handle from the inside to block it. My worst nightmare.

I jumped up and tried to move the handle with my paws, to push it down ... but I kept slipping. It was simply stuck.

Inside the bedroom I could hear Pearl hissing, then Julia's choked voice pleading with André to see reason.

"Don't hurt me!" she finally cried.

I barked like a lunatic. Someone in the neighboring villas had to hear me, and come to my rescue, before this madman did something worse to Julia. Because she didn't return his supposed love....

Again I threw myself against the door, but the damn thing was massive. I tried to push the handle down with my muzzle, but only sprained my neck muscles.

Then, when I was already despairing, the door suddenly popped open as if by itself.

Pearl? She must have somehow managed to knock over the chair and open it for me. But how was that possible? She was so small ... and up there on the bed when I spotted her.

No time to think about that now. I charged into the room and was next to her on the mattress in two giant leaps.

Pearl was just about to plunge her tiny teeth into André's exposed Achilles tendon. As she did so, she hissed like a fully-grown jaguar—but André was barely impressed. He kicked out with his foot and hurled his death-defying little attacker, who had tried to come to Julia's aid, away from him.

Luckily Pearl landed on all fours and still on the mattress so she wasn't hurt, but this mistreatment of my poor pipsqueak finally turned me into a ravaging wolf.

I tensed my muscles and threw myself with all my might at André. I tore him away from Julia, and only now saw that the knife blade was in his hand again, but I didn't flinch for long. I bit into his forearm so hard that he cried out and dropped the knife.

He moved aside, but I attacked once more and came to rest on top of him, my muzzle very close to his face. Growling wildly, I bared my teeth.

He gave up resisting, howling and cursing in pain, but no longer fighting me.

"The cell phone," I called out to Pearl. "Take it to Julia. She needs to call the police!"

The pipsqueak didn't need to be told twice. Out of the corner of my eye I could see her nimbly climbing up onto the dresser and trying to grab the phone with her snout, just like I would have done. But the thing was much too big for her.

What did she do then? She solved the problem in her very best feline manner. She gave the phone a swinging push with her paw and watched it fly off the dresser!

She hadn't aimed perfectly: the phone landed just beside the bed on the floor, but was fortunately sturdy enough to survive the fall. Julia only had to roll to the side, bend over the edge of the bed and stretch her fingers to reach it.

She dialed 911 and I bared my teeth once more for safety's sake—so that André, who was still buried beneath me, wouldn't get any ideas. This time I would sink my teeth into his neck *before* he could grab me like a helpless puppy and throw me out of the room! And he probably understood that I was serious.

32

Over the next few days, we learned more and more details from Oskar as the true frightening extent of André's madness was revealed. Everything he had done to frame Tristan for murder and to finally get rid of the hated competitor who owned Julia's love once and for all.

André had written the anonymous letters to Julia himself, to plant the idea in her head that her supposed suicide at the Black Cliffs Hotel had in fact been a plot by her unfaithful husband.

And it had been André who'd spiked Julia's orange juice with Steven's antihypertensives. However, he'd made the dosage low enough that Julia's life would not have been in any real danger—as he'd repeatedly affirmed during his endless interrogations by Oskar Nüring. Presumably this was true because, after all, the man was a nurse and knew a lot about drugs.

André had also carried out the second attack with the pillow himself, taking care to only briefly cut off Julia's air supply and thus not permanently harm her. He'd disguised his voice, chosen words that fit her relationship with Tristan, and when he'd finally let go of Julia he'd disappeared to the side of the bed where he'd been sitting before. In the darkness of the room, that had not been a problem. Then, in a flash, he had begun acting as if he had just woken from a deep sleep, completely befuddled and apparently awakened by Julia's cry for help, which he himself had permitted during his pretended suffocation of her.

Likewise it had been André who had previously stirred the sleeping drugs into the hot chocolate that most of those present at the villa had drunk—a precautionary measure that was supposed to facilitate his diabolical plan.

It took a little while longer for André to admit to the murder of Edward Laymon as well.

He had presented his old friend, whose petty criminal nature he knew very well, as a detective to Julia and used him to feed her fake evidence of her husband's infidelity. She should see what a womanizer Tristan truly was and finally turn her back on him.

André would have been there to comfort her and open her eyes to see the man who truly loved her. Then it might not have been necessary to take more radical steps and frame Tristan as a murderer. But Julia had held fast to her husband.

Moreover, Edward Laymon had put a spoke in André's wheel, because when he'd come to the island and played his role as a detective in front of Julia, he'd understood the perfidious game for which André had hired him. However, he had not gone to Julia or Tristan with this realization, but had tried to extort a much higher fee from André than originally agreed. But with this he had signed his own death warrant.

We were also able to solve perhaps the greatest mystery of all, on the very first day after André's arrest. Who on earth had opened the bedroom door for me that night, during the decisive fight with the lunatic nurse after he had so elegantly dumped me out in the hallway?

If I hadn't managed to return to Julia's bedroom, and incapacitated André thanks to the element of surprise, she might not have survived his wrath.

So how had I gotten into the room? That very night, right after André had been arrested, Pearl had asked me how I had managed to open the door. She knew as well as I did that a chair had been blocking the handle.

All I could tell her was that the door had magically sprung open all by itself at the crucial moment—an extremely unsatisfactory explanation.

We had stayed with Victoria at Julia's villa for the rest of the night so she wouldn't have to be alone and we could help her recover from the shock she had suffered.

When we ran into the kitchen in the morning to inspect room service's early breakfast delivery, Pearl did something very strange. She didn't turn straight to the table to examine the food and make sure a portion of salmon had been ordered for her. Instead, she squinted up at the countertop next to the sink, where once again a bowl was sitting out, probably from yesterday. I could smell that it contained the same cereal, as we already knew, and Pearl probably could too. The slightly sweet scent rose to both of our noses.

"The little boy's favorite," she stated, suddenly looking very thoughtful.

The salmon I sniffed on the table behind me was giving off an exquisite smell; it had to be of the best quality, but Pearl was squatting there like a bronze statue, staring off into nowhere.

"Are you okay, Tiny?" I asked worriedly.

"The door of Julia's bedroom burst open at a crucial moment," she said abruptly, "as if by magic—that's how you put it, isn't it?"

"Yes?"

"It occurred to me that I saw a shadow; I remember that now. Something small that pulled the chair out from under the handle and then disappeared through the door right after you rushed in. I wasn't sure ... I was, um, distracted. André had just fought off my third or fourth attack, which disappointed me quite a bit, I must admit. It was just so easy for him—"

"You did your best," I tried to comfort her. "That's all that matters."

"Nice of you," she said. She looked so broodingly distracted that she didn't even defend her honor as a fighter.

"What I'm getting at, Athos," she said instead, "is I think I know who came to our rescue at the crucial moment—who opened the door for you so you could save Julia."

She nimbly clambered up the handles of the kitchen

cabinets, and reached the countertop where the bowl was. She sniffed it.

"I think the little boy who likes to eat this porridge so much was the one I saw by the door," she explained to me. "He was the shadow that let you back into the room. But how could he be so incredibly fast? And who, by the great cat goddess, is he really?"

"We have to find out," I said stoutly.

33

Just at that very moment, Julia and Victoria came into the kitchen. Both women smiled when they spotted the tiny one on the countertop.

Victoria patted me on the head and said, "Good Athos, good dog!" I'd probably earned the spontaneous praise because I had left the dishes on the table untouched. I could easily have reached them without jumping on any of the furniture.

But I had an idea. I walked straight up to Pearl, put my front paws on the countertop, and gave the bowl of cereal a nudge with my muzzle. Then I yelped loudly—and repeated the maneuver.

We had observed the strange boy eating from this porridge earlier, and it had even appeared that Julia had prepared the dish especially and had deliberately left it for him in the kitchen or on her bedside table.

With my nudge-maneuver and yelping, I'd managed to draw Julia's and Victoria's attention to the porridge. Promptly, the two duly did what I'd hoped they would.

Julia said, "Oh, you're welcome to eat it, my brave rescuers, but I'm not sure you'll like it. Look, over here on the table—I've ordered some yummy bites for you two."

And Victoria said, pointing at the porridge bowl, "What is it? A special food that you make for yourself?

Cereal grits?"

Julia suddenly smiled. She seemed a little embarrassed.

"Oh," she said, "it's not for me. It's ... you'll think I'm crazy, Victoria. A superstitious old hag."

"You're hardly an old hag." Victoria laughed. "And you're not the crazy one in your circle..."

The corners of Julia's mouth twisted. "Don't remind me of him—please. I still can't believe that my gentle, devoted nurse was really a psychopath who..."

She broke off and took a deep breath.

"So, the porridge," she continued, "is an old superstition I picked up from my mother. She came from right here on Sylt, you know. When I was a little kid, she often read me fairy tales and legends, and one of the stories was about a kind of goblin she called Puk. Something like a guardian spirit, related to the Puck that William Shakespeare wrote about in his *A Midsummer Night's Dream*."

"Oh, yes," Victoria agreed. "The legends are not only told here in northern Germany or in England. In Austria we also know such stories, of goblins and trolls, of brownies and other nature spirits, who can help or harm people. Beautiful tales for children, I think."

"But my mother really believed in the existence of this Puk," Julia said. "When she had problems or was afraid of something, she would always cook up some porridge with lots of butter. She claimed it was the little Puk's favorite food. She would then serve him the porridge and ask that he protect her in return."

Julia smiled pensively as she reminisced about her mother in this way. "This ritual, cooking porridge for the brownie, relaxed her I think. And now when I came here to the island, and that first anonymous letter showed up, I remembered my mother and those old stories. It gave me comfort, you know? Mom is long gone, but when I cook this porridge like she used to, I feel protected. It's childish, I know. I've made this porridge several times in the last few days and put it here in the kitchen or in my bedroom to attract the Puk. And I could have sworn someone ate some of it, Victoria!"

"Maybe Athos or Pearl have a taste for it after all," said our two-legged. She returned Julia's smile. Then she inspected the inviting food that room service had brought. "Shall we have something to eat? I'm starving."

"We're supposed to have eaten that porridge?" Pearl asked me with a wrinkled nose. "How can she think we'd even touch such mush?"

But at the same time we looked at each other triumphantly.

"This Puk ... he's not just a legend," I said. "We've actually seen him."

"And he more than earned his porridge," Pearl said. "True, he did fail to protect Julia's supposed detective. That's probably why he was out there with the body, tearing his hair in grief. And when we were watching him here in the house, in Julia's bedroom, he knocked over the orange juice because maybe André had already mixed some of the drug into the bottle. Probably the Puk was watching him secretly and of course assumed that he really wanted to kill Julia. The brownie could not have known that the madman only wanted to get Tristan out of the way. But in the end, the little one managed to protect Julia against her real enemy and possibly even saved her life—because who knows what André would have done to her in the end if she had continued to reject him and thus irritated him to the point of outright rage. It was Puk who opened the bedroom door for you last night, and by doing so he may have saved my life too. Because I would have continued to attack André, of course, and he ... was a bit bigger and stronger than me."

"A bit, yes," I said. "But not half as brave."

Pearl licked my nose with her tiny pink tongue.

What remains to be told about this sad chain of events? Tristan was, of course, released from prison, and when he learned the whole terrible story surrounding André and his atrocities, he reacted in a truly unexpected way. He gave notice to his secretary, with whom he had in fact cheated, and remembered his marriage vows.

He contritely asked Julia to forgive him.

"I didn't protect you," he reproached himself, "not at the Black Cliffs and much less this time. I'm so glad nothing happened to you. The idea of losing you, dear heart..." He pressed his lips together and shook his head. "Do you think you could give me another chance? I beg of you."

"I will," Julia said, after hesitating for a moment and then sighing heavily. "You may be a bit of a bastard, but at least you're not a murderer. And you're *my* bastard, and I love you, stupid as it may sound. But please don't call me *dear heart* anymore, okay? I used to like it, but now I can't bear it anymore. It reminds me of that psychopath who put a pillow over my face pretending to be you ... and I fell for it."

Bianca, with great remorse—which I nevertheless thought was feigned—returned the stolen jewels to Julia and tore up her contract with Tristan concerning her share in the Harrington hotel chain.

In return, Julia refrained from pressing charges for the jewelry theft. She wanted to finally have peace, she said, and never see Bianca again. Not even in court.

All we heard from Celeste and Scarlett was that they were unharmed and well. Neither of them seemed to want to return to Steven or Jude.

And as far as the hotel empire was concerned, Steven officially chose Tristan as his successor, but he at least had the decency to appoint his brother in a leading position in the company and to sign over a part of the shares to him.

I still had a debt to repay to *bro* fox, and so in the next few days, when I finally found the leisure to roam around Sylt at night again, I brought him the promised delicacies from Victoria's kitchen.

I also had to tell him all about the recent murder

case.

"Man, my dude, it's sooo cool to know a real police dog," he commented enthusiastically.

I would have liked to introduce him to Pearl, who would have been a police cat in his eyes, but she preferred to hold down the fort on Victoria's sofa. There she indulged extensively in the consumption of salmon, personal beauty care and the high art of the siesta.

We were both looking forward to Christmas, now, when we'd be going to Vienna with Victoria to visit her boyfriend Tim. Which—at least if Pearl had her way—didn't mean that we couldn't add Oskar Nüring to our family pack as one of our humans in the future.

More from Alex Wagner

If you enjoy snooping around with Athos and Pearl, why not try my other mystery series, too?

Penny Küfer Investigates—cozy mysteries full of old world charm.
Penny only has two legs, but she's a feisty and clever young detective.

Murder in Antiquity—a historical mystery series from the Roman Empire.
Join shady Germanic merchant Thanar and his clever slave Layla in their backwater frontier town, and on their travels to see the greatest sights of the ancient world. Meet legionaries, gladiators, barbarians, druids and Christians—and the most ruthless killers in the Empire!

About the author

Alex Wagner lives with her husband and 'partner in crime' near Vienna, Austria. From her writing chair she has a view of an old ruined castle, which helps her to dream up the most devious murder plots.

Alex writes mysteries set in the most beautiful locations in Europe, and in popular holiday destinations. If you love to read Agatha Christie and other authors from the Golden Age of mystery fiction, you will enjoy her stories.

www.alexwagner.at
www.facebook.com/AlexWagnerMysteryWriter

Copyright © 2023 Alexandra Wagner
Publisher: Alexandra Wagner

All rights reserved. This book or any portion thereof may not be reproduced or used in any manner whatsoever without the express written permission of the publisher, except for the use of brief quotations in a book review.
The characters in this book are entirely fictional. Any resemblance to actual persons living or dead is entirely coincidental.

Cover design: Estella Vukovic
Editor: Tarryn Thomas

Printed in Great Britain
by Amazon